The
Ditchcrawler

by Dermot Moloney

Q

First Published in Great Britain in 2024

7 Grape Lane, Petergate, York YO1 7HU
Tel: +44 (0)1904 635967
Email: info@quacks.info
Website: radiusonline.info

Quacks Books is an imprint of Radius Publishing Ltd

A CIP catalogue record for this book is available from the British Library.

ISBN: 978-1-912728-83-1

Set on a page size of 176mm x 250mm printed by offset lithography on one hundred gsm chosen for its sustainability.

Disclaimer
This is a work of fiction. Any similarities between characters or plot and real people and events are purely coincidental.

Dedication

In memory of my father, who built a boat in our dining room and couldn't get it out through the French windows, and my mother who saw the funny side.

Salt Head Island

Cockle Hole

Boverey Marsh

2020

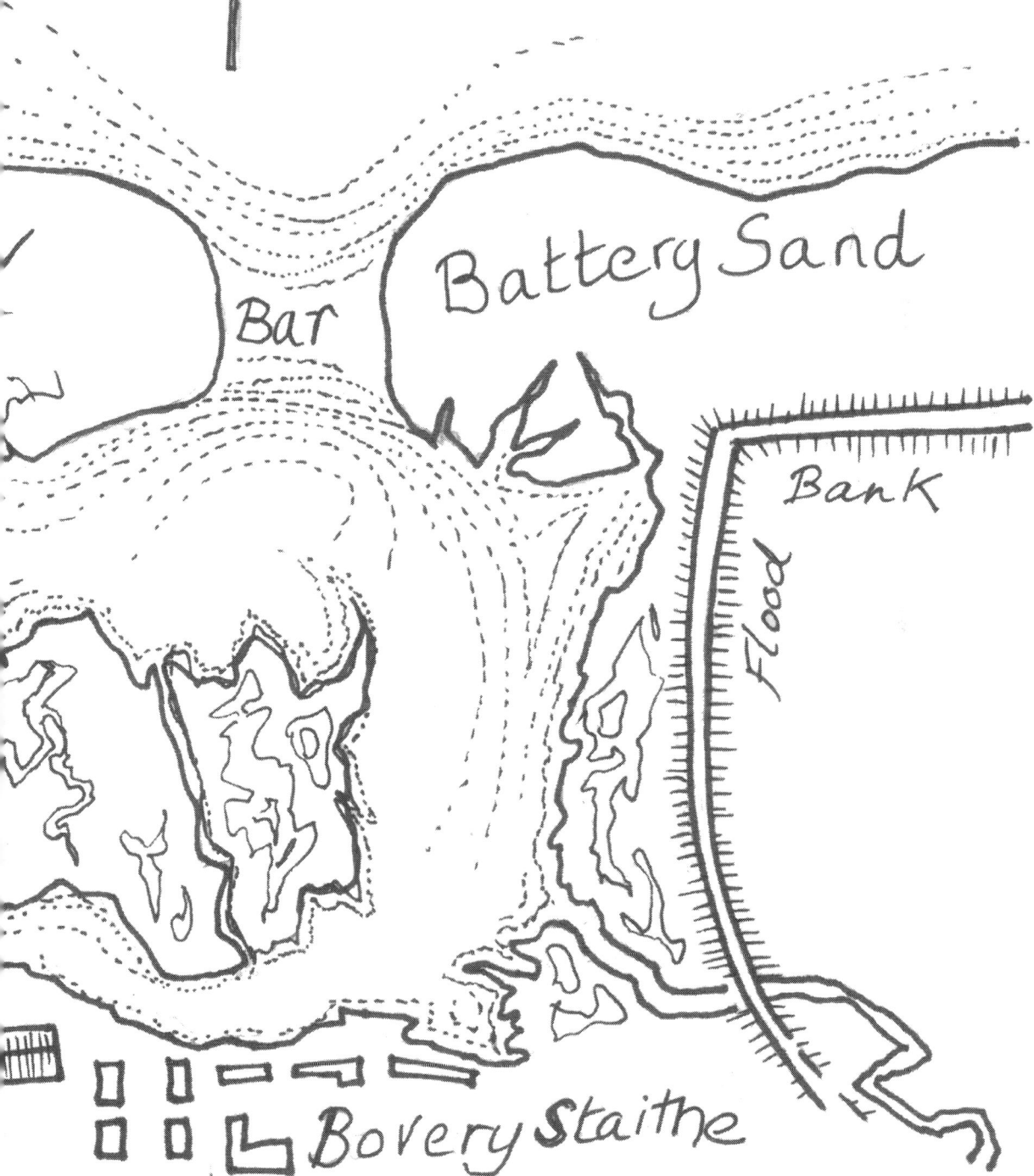

PREFACE

Evan Price and Peter Rufford don't know each other from Adam, but each receives an unsigned invitation to a remote pub in a part of England neither has ever visited. Each has a reason to comply, and here, deep in the Fens, they get wind of a mutual acquaintance who presents them with an opportunity to assist him in an investigation into a centuries-old legend relating in some way to his own more recent past.

His motives are opaque and his manner vague, but his guests quickly come to realise that he really does need their help: they just can't quite figure out how or why.

Enthralled by a situation which constantly throws up more questions than it answers, they are drawn into the heart of the mystery and embark upon a strange odyssey through landscapes and seascapes whose lonely beauty seems to conceal an existential threat … just as their host seems increasingly prone to conceal the truth about the very story he says he wants them to unravel.

Eventually, the summer ends with storms – both literal and metaphorical – and the drama plays out in the pounding surf and shifting sands of a fragile island harbouring a fragile secret on north Norfolk's beleaguered coast.

AUTHOR'S NOTE

I wrote what follows well over a generation ago and I suppose it is the first major story I managed to complete in very early adulthood. At the time I called it a novel, but it isn't anything like long enough for that. It certainly isn't a *short* story either, so the rather old fashioned term *novella* will have to do. This is appropriate as it is in some ways a rather old fashioned story.

Re-reading it for my own amusement, I was gratified to find it rather better written than I had remembered, which triggered a conviction that I really ought to do something with it. The temptation, of course, was to re-write it completely; eradicating clichés and padding out the action in order to produce a proper full-length novel. But then it wouldn't be what it is and would cease to belong to the phase of my life in which it was conceived.

Nor have I modernised the action. There are no laptops or mobile phones in evidence here. Indeed, the original MS is a dog-eared typescript in a torn cardboard folder. There is also a kind of naivety about the main characters which might seem out of place post 9/11 or Covid 19, but which I now find almost charming and wish to retain. Of course I do have my pride. Thus I *have* made a number of corrections; eliminating an embarrassing grammatical error here or re-balancing a clumsy sentence there. I have also resolved a couple of direct contradictions of plot, but mere improbabilities and co-incidences I have left alone. To iron them out now would be as awkwardly intrusive as the introduction of personal computers and other such devices.

It is what it is: an adventure story; and I happily acknowledge that readers familiar with the genre may well detect the influence of Erskine Childers and Arthur Ransom among others. For me it is something else too … a kind of memoir of the two summer holidays which inspired it, taken on that part of the Norfolk coast now sometimes known as *Chelsea on Sea* thanks to its popularity with the Metropolitan Elite. But four decades ago it was still an undiscovered country, known only to its natives; hardy campers, enthusiastic ornithologists and passionate dinghy sailors. Even today the glittering gin palaces of the *nouveaux riche* can't quite get up the myriad creeks and into the shallow lagoons threading the vast marshes behind the dunes, and when I make my not-infrequent visits to this place I am still moved to the core by its lonely and truly *awful* beauty.

I am no longer exactly certain when I started to draught or even think about this story, but there are one or two pieces of internal evidence which may be of assistance if you are the kind of reader who likes to burrow into these things. If so, I suggest you begin by looking into the survival (or otherwise!) of a certain seaside pier …

York 2024

ONE

It is an odd tale I tell, but no less true for that, and its curious beginning is an appropriate harbinger of its middle and its end. Like an Edwardian school story, it concerns a sequence of events crammed into the final sun-drenched week or two of a summer holiday. Only we were not school children and – for me at least - it was the *only* fortnight of the holiday. However, the sun did indeed shine, and that was something, I suppose, considering the storm which was to break at its conclusion.

The Celtic West I know well, living as I do in the outskirts of Hay-on-Wye, deep in the Welsh Marches. Thus Wales, Cornwall and Cumbria were all firmly on my radar by the time I received the mysterious letter inviting me to explore new ground in the Saxon East. So it was sheer curiosity no doubt, which led me to comply with its almost outrageous demands. Anyway, Saturday August 17th found me coaxing the old Morris Minor up out of the woody valleys of Herefordshire and on through the pastoral idyll of south Warwickshire.

It was all so very English, in an American sort of way: the village greens with black and white cottages groaning under their mountains of thatch; the glinting duck ponds reflecting a war memorial or a venerable oak; grey-pink sandstone churches peeping through screens of yew and beech, and dark copses crowning hillocks and ridges almost white with standing corn. *Shakespeare's England*, of course ... fit for a million picture postcards.

I despise motorways and A roads, and towns are to be avoided like the plague. Therefore whenever I intend a long journey I buy all the Ordnance Survey sheets my route will cross and work out a meandering progress through the landscape. My friends shudder at the cost of my petrol, but then they drink more beer than I do.

By mid afternoon I had reached Leicestershire without seeing a big town and began to bear slightly southwards down the long dip slope into another England and, by four o'clock, I was deep in the Fens where my story truly begins.

If I had to choose between the mountains and the plain I would undoubtedly choose the mountains, but the extraordinary openness of these watery levels almost gave me the same sense of absolute freedom I derive from a high and rocky peak. I had never been to the Fens before and was soon mesmerised by this seemingly endless *prairie* of gilded grain sheeting away to an almost treeless horizon. Sword-like watercourses criss-crossed the entire landscape with uncompromising regularity. These too contributed to the uncanny sense of *otherness* and isolation.

I gave Peterborough a very wide berth and threaded my way into the northern extremities of Cambridgeshire, embarking on what I assumed was to be the last leg of my journey, eventually locating my destination after a sequence of delightful detours in order to find my way over the numerous canals, or *drains* as they are called hereabouts. Shortly before six, I spotted the flinty tower of a parish church to my left and - after negotiating two more small bridges – I rolled into the pub car park at Bradwell St Helen.

So great was my fascination with the landscape that I had almost forgotten the letter in the glove compartment, and the old coin I was instructed to give to the landlord of the *Six Horseshoes*. Quite why I had to give him an obsolete half crown I had no idea, but it had come with the letter and the letter was clear (and unclear) enough.

Retrieving the letter from the glove compartment and grabbing my small rucksack from the back seat, I stepped out onto the crunchy gravel and looked up at the pub.

The *Six Horseshoes* was clearly the only pub in the village. It was not a particularly beautiful building but it was pleasant enough: plain provincial Regency or perhaps early Victorian, with a pedimented doorway and four sash windows positioned with the symmetry of a child's drawing. The brickwork was heavily whitewashed and the peeling signboard hung motionless in the hot, still air. The door was ajar and there was one other vehicle in the car park, a battered blue mini. Presumably the pub had been open for a while, but I had no idea what the local licensing hours were like. Perhaps nobody bothered to check up this far out in the sticks!

I went in.

Feeling once more the unease I had felt on receiving the letter, I nodded towards the knot of old men in the public bar and made for the counter. Then, convinced that, at best, he would be as baffled as I was, or, at worst, take me for a complete idiot; I produced the half crown and placed it before the landlord.

"Good evening," I said. "I believe I am to give you this."

He looked down at the coin for a moment, without touching it. "Are you Evan Price?"

"Yes," I said. "How did you know?"

"Well, you're not Peter Rufford now, are you?" he replied with a faint smile as he began to draw a pint into a thick , dimpled glass with a good old fashioned handle.

"Who's Peter Rufford?"

"Well, I don't rightly know *who* he is," said the landlord, topping up the pint. "But he's over there in the corner. He gave me half a crown too."

I looked round and saw someone I hadn't noticed when I'd come in. He was about my age and was on his own at a corner table on which, beside his glass, lay a familiar buff envelope. I had started to move towards him when the landlord called me back."

"Don't forget your beer, sir."

"Mine?"

"Well it's paid for. Didn't you know?"

"No."

"Strange," he said, almost to himself. "Mr Rufford didn't know either."

By this time the figure in the corner had guessed that my presence here had something to do with his and he waved the brown envelope as I approached.

"Did you send this?" he asked. His accent was vaguely northern.

"No. Did you send this?" I replied, pulling out my own letter as I sat down.

"Let's see it," he said, and we both opened our respective envelopes and extracted their contents, spreading them side by side on the copper topped table.

They were identical. Typed and unsigned. They said simply:-

Repair to the Six Horseshoes, Bradwell St Helen, Cambs. on the evening of August 17th and give the landlord the enclosed coin. Make sure you have taken at least two weeks' holiday and do not worry about accommodation. Just bring outdoor clothes and a toothbrush. Further instructions will be received at the aforesaid hostelry.

We looked up and wondered what we had in common … which was very little, physically. He was tall, fair and wore reading glasses whereas I was short, dark and keen sighted at any range. He seemed friendly enough, but then we were both trying to solve the same problem so hostility wasn't going to help either of us.

We exchanged biographies: dates and places of birth; education; recent holidays and circles of friends etc. As far as we could see, it was unlikely that our paths had ever crossed. Yet there had to be someone or something which connected us, but the only thing we seemed to have in common was that we were both relatively recent graduates … though his degree was in physical geography and geology, whereas mine was firmly rooted in the humanities.

We mulled over the facts of our arrival in Bradwell St Helen for some time and slowly drank our beer, toasting our anonymous benefactor.

"There really *can* only be one solution," I said, not for the first time. "We really *must* have a mutual acquaintance who wants us both in the same place at the same time."

"*Here*," said Rufford. "And *now*. So let's hope it's a friend."

I glanced nervously at the door, racking my brains for a connection. Peter Rufford was a junior surveyor from Lancaster. He had taken his degree at Newcastle and returned to his home town to work with a long established local land agency. I had been born and brought up near Hereford and taken my degree at the University of Warwick … which is actually in Coventry for some strange reason. As far as I knew, I had never known anyone who had lived or studied in Newcastle, and I had only once visited Lancaster, en route to the Lake District with my parents some years ago.

Peter suddenly seemed to think of something: "You're a journalist, right? Did you do any specific training for that? After Warwick, I mean?"

Of course! How stupid of me.

"Yes! Sorry ... I should have mentioned it. I did a six month crash course at Cardiff Polly. Why?"

"Well it's just that an old school friend of mine wanted to be a journalist. He *did* go somewhere in Wales to train but didn't like it and gave up. Went into something else. I don't know what."

"What was his name?"

"Mike. Michael O'Brien."

Light dawned and I grinned broadly, slapping both hands on the table top, rattling the by now empty glasses. "Liverpool Irish ... and proud of it!"

Rufford's jaw dropped: "You do know him then?"

"Yes. Well ... just a little bit. He wasn't there long, as you say, but we shared digs and got on well enough. But I thought he was from Liverpool, not Lancaster."

Peter smiled: "He was born in Liverpool, but he moved up to Lancaster when he was about fourteen, so we met at secondary school. He didn't mention school much then?"

"Not that I remember. Come to think of it, he said very little about his background. At least not about his own background. He went on a lot about Ireland, though. But I don't think he'd ever been."

"Sounds like our Mike," laughed Pete. "And you're right. He'd never been to Ireland, but everyone was het up about the Troubles one way or another, whether they were Irish or not. He used to go on *Troops Out* demos and got pelted with eggs and stones by local skinheads."

"Did you stay in touch?" I asked.

"Just Christmas cards and the odd letter, until about half way through university. He went to York, by the way. Then they got thinner and eventually fizzled out altogether. I only heard about the Cardiff episode second hand. I did go round to his parents' home once but they'd moved on. The new people gave me an address in Keswick but I got no reply when I wrote so I suppose they'd moved again. Thought about driving up there but never got round to it. You know how it is."

I did indeed. We all so easily lose touch with people we swear will be our boon companions forever.

"I did like him," I said. "And was sorry when he left. But there was something odd about him."

"Well he *was* Irish," said Peter, with a grin.

"Liverpool Irish anyway. But it wasn't that. I'm mostly Welsh after all."

"What then?"

"He seemed to take everything so seriously. Not that he didn't have a sense of humour, but he was … well … like Macbeth trying to play Falstaff."

"My Shakespeare's not too good I'm afraid," said Peter.

"Sorry. It's just that however cheerful he seemed, there was always something in his eyes. Fear. Anger, perhaps. I don't know."

"I know what you mean," Peter agreed. "He was a good entertainer but he never let the audience backstage."

"Exactly!" I said, pleased at his extension of my theatrical metaphor.

"It's probably a Liverpool-Irish thing: constantly having to reconcile two identities and all that. More beer?"

I took our glasses and walked to the bar. The landlord pulled the pints but shook his head as I produced my wallet.

"Open cheque," he grunted. "Whatever you drink now plus dinner, bed and breakfast for two. What's it all about, anyway?"

I blinked at him. "If you don't know, we certainly don't. You said an open cheque … it must have been signed?"

He hesitated a moment before replying: "Er … yes, it was. But the letter with it said I wasn't to identify the writer."

"Didn't you find that suspicious?"

"Of course I did. Spoke to the local bobby about it too. Got his Chief Superintendent to contact the bank which confirmed his account existed and was healthy enough."

"So unless he's using a false name," I said. "He's not a crook."

"Who says it's a *he*?" asked the landlord, with a slight shrug.

"You did. You said *his* account."

"Ah. So I did. Well never mind. Anyway, an open cheque's not to be sniffed at if it's kosher. So, when you're ready, I'll give you a menu for tonight and if you bring your luggage in I'll show you to your rooms. When you've drunk up, of course, No hurry."

"Thanks," I said, taking the glasses back to the table.

Peter looked thoughtful. "You know, these letters may have come from someone else entirely."

"No," I replied firmly. "The more I think about it, the more I'm sure it's him. Call it instinct if you want. A *hunch*, may be … but I'm certain."

"So we've got the *who*," said Peter. "Next up: the *why*."

Why indeed? Well, the letters had said we would receive further instructions at the *Six Horseshoes* so we sat and drank our beer and waited. The promised menu – as I'd expected – was typical pub grub: chips with everything, but that was welcome enough after a long drive. As we ate, conversation turned general and the strange thing was that I began to feel as if I'd known Peter for years and soon we were talking like old friends. Perhaps this always happens when total strangers reminisce about a mutual comrade: I don't know.

Presently the landlord came over to take the dead glasses and dropped yet another buff envelope on the table. It was addressed – by hand this time – simply to *Peter and Evan*. We both stared at it for a moment, giving each other the chance to open it.

"You do it," said Peter, so I took it and fumbled with the well-gummed flap. Like our previous letters it was typed and unsigned:

By now you must be very perplexed indeed, but don't worry. You will spend tonight at the Six Horseshoes in the ample care of Mr Sherriff, the landlord, whom I confess I have never met but of whom I have heard nothing but good reports. Then, tomorrow morning, repair to Bradwell Hard for 10.00 AM and await the good ship "Samphire", upon which vessel I shall explain everything … or almost everything. You may leave your vehicles with Mr Sherriff: they will be quite safe in the stable yard. I hope you remembered the toothbrushes!

"Curiouser and curiouser," I couldn't help but say.

We carried our own plates back to the bar and went to take our cars round into the stable yard as instructed, leaving the keys with the landlord just in case he had to move them for any reason. Back inside, we humped our rucksacks upstairs and were shown to our bare but clean rooms. Mine was at the back and commanded a west facing view across the flat, dusty fields, crimson under a crimson sky, with an horizon broken only by a distant line of scant black poplars. Peter's looked east, where the sky was a deeper shade of red as the light drained out of it. Here there was no horizon at all because the fields were fading into the oncoming night … except for a tiny point of golden light, steadily focussed like a fallen, earthbound star.

"Ely Cathedral," said Mr Sherriff. "Lit up for the tourists. Wouldn't like their electric bill, that's for sure! Well, goodnight to you both."

We stood on the hot landing and listened his retreating footsteps on the creaky stairs.

"The really weird thing about all this," I said, "is that we've both bothered to come at all … answer the summons, so to speak. It's crazy! We receive anonymous letters telling us to drop everything and come out to this desolate place for no obvious reason … and we do!"

"By the way, was it hard to get the time off?" he asked.

"Actually no. I showed my editor the letter and he got quite excited and suggested that if there was a good story in it he might not even regard the time as holiday. Though quite how relevant it's likely to be for a local rag in Hay-on-Wye I can't imagine. How about you?"

He looked down for a moment.

"Well …" he began slowly. "I haven't taken holiday. My allocation's used up and the boss wouldn't extend it."

"But you're here …" I coaxed, unsure how delicate this was going to be.

"Yes," he said sharply. "I resigned."

For a minute there was nothing I could say, and when I *could* speak I muttered some platitude about hoping it would all work out for him."

"So do I," he said, turning into his room.

Later, in bed, I thought things over for the hundredth time and continued to get nowhere. Whatever had drawn us both to Bradwell St Helen must have been a powerful force and for the first time my general unease began to mutate into something else. Plain old common-or-garden fear. I thought of the surrounding fields, vast and eerie in the silver moonlight now. This landscape which had intrigued me so much as I'd driven across it seemed suddenly hostile, and those glinting watercourses held nothing but threats.

TWO

Dawn on Sunday broke in the traditional manner with a cockerel shrieking under the window, which cheered me up somewhat. Bright sunlight flooded the room and, best of all, the indescribably blissful aroma of sizzling bacon drifted up from below. Breakfast tasted as good as it smelt, and afterwards we spread the appropriate ordnance sheet on the cleared table and sought Bradwell Hard. It turned out to be two cottages and a slipway about a mile from the village on a long straight canal called Van Reuygen's Drain.

Apparently this watery wasteland had been reclaimed for agriculture by gangs of ingenious but locally unpopular Dutchmen in the middle years of the 17th century. They employed their brilliant engineering techniques to produce some the richest arable land in England, making a great deal of money for their aristocratic investors whilst ruining the local economy which had depended on fishing and fowling for centuries. The native population, the so-called *Fen Tigers*, were left destitute and rose in revolt. Dykes were breached, sluices wrecked, shots fired and throats cut in the dark. The Dutch won, of course, having established armed camps across the region and were always able to call for backup from the militias commanded by their land-owning investors. (This may have been *Cromwell Country* but the land owners still ruled the roost, even in the brave new Republic!) Van Reuygen's Drain was obviously one of the fruits of their labour.

Unsure whether we would be returning to the village again that day, we took our rucksacks with us when we set out on foot for the Hard.

It was an interesting place if you liked boats. A clutter of sailing dinghies was drawn up on the slipway, and a line of cabin cruisers lay moored to pontoons along the bank. A few of these were once-elegant wooden classics, but looking a bit shabby now. Bradwell Hard was not Henley-on-Thames after all. The rest were modern fibreglass, but even some of these were looking decidedly the worse for wear. We read their names carefully: *Tudor Rose; Fen Tiger; Polar Star* etc… but there was no sign of a *Samphire* among them.

The Drain stretched away in opposite directions, unerringly straight into the south west to our right, and the north east to our left. It was constrained between high levees of grass-grown earth, and from the bank top on our side you could see a good mile of clear water either way. Assuming *Samphire* was coming under her own steam, so to speak, and not being trailed overland, we should have no difficulty spotting her well in advance.

In the event we heard her before we saw her: a faint buzz gradually strengthening into a decidedly mechanical putter away to our right. We turned and shaded our eyes as she came into view, little more than a dot on the water, like a small pebble on a mirror. I produced my binoculars and brought her into focus. I could just make out that she was a small cabin yacht – probably wooden – with a single mast. As she drew closer it became clear that she was towing a dinghy in her wake. A solitary figure crouched in the cockpit, one hand on the tiller of the outboard, whose putter was fast becoming a throaty clatter like the sound of an old British motorbike. The dinghy on the towline was well laden, her contents lashed down under a green tarp.

Now I could read the name: "*Samphire!* I wonder what it means?"

Peter shrugged: "Well this is it, Evan. You can always ask O'Brien … or whoever it turns out to be."

I nodded and let the binoculars hang by their strap. The skipper cut the motor and the boat swung in towards an empty pontoon at precisely ten o'clock, bumping gently against the rubber tyre fenders. She was about twenty feet long, clinker built and clearly quite old. Pre-war anyway. The cabin, with its miniature brass-bound portholes, dipped towards the tiny foredeck, and a rust-red sail was furled around a spar lying on the coachroof. I breathed a sigh of relief: she was lug-rigged, which meant no boom. I'd done enough small boat sailing in my time to appreciate the value of a hard hat! Lugsails are unusual on craft of this type, but so much about this entire situation was unusual that little could surprise me now.

We were hailed – heartily and by name – from the cockpit. We crossed the slipway and climbed onto the pontoon in order to take her lines and tie her up. We were neither of us in any doubt now that the skipper was Michael O'Brien, and we climbed aboard as bidden. Neither of us said anything at first, but stood side by side in the gently rocking cockpit and waited for him to explain himself. He expressed no surprise that we had appeared on cue (which was somehow a little un-nerving) but welcomed us aboard and invited us below.

"Not until you tell us what this is all about," said Peter, with uncharacteristic firmness. I nodded in support.

O'Brien laughed loudly: "It's a long story, boys, and I don't know all of it myself yet. Come below and take seat and I'll do my best. Coffee's up."

We shrugged slightly and followed him as he pushed the tiny sliding doghouse forward and ducked through the companion way. *Below* proved to be just two steps down into a very small saloon, with a berth each side of a narrow table. Pete and I sat down opposite each other and O'Brien sat next to me. It would have been impossible to have stood, but it was certainly cosy. A steaming enamel coffee pot and three tin mugs stood on the table.

"Black only, I'm afraid," said our host. "Can't keep milk fresh at this time of year, but there's sugar if you want it."

We were happy with black and he gestured us to help ourselves.

"Well," he said at last. "Where do we begin?"

We looked at him blankly.

"It's like this …" he began but paused, playing with his mug, rotating it in his hands. I took the opportunity to study his face, to see if it had changed at all, but I could detect no difference since Cardiff. His hair and beard were still as red, and like all Irishmen he had the look of both king and peasant stamped on his brow, but his accent was non-descript … not even particularly Scouse. Like Peter, he might possibly be taken for a Mancunian, but only just.

Swallowing a mouthful of coffee he nodded suddenly and continued: "I have a job to do and I want your help."

"*Want*, or *need?*" I asked.

"Both," he replied. "In any case, you might find it rewarding. *You*, particularly, Evan."

"Because I'm a journalist?"

"Maybe."

Peter fixed him with what I suspect was as stern a look as he could muster.

"That's all very well for Evan," he said. "But I was left with no choice but to give up my job for this. I can't even sign on because I'm here, aren't I? So, to put it crudely: *what's in it for me?*"

O'Brien looked genuinely shocked for a moment.

"I see," he said slowly. "Well … consider yourself – as of now – employed by me for a while. Of course I can't *pay* you anything just yet, but you've got free bed and …" he tapped his mug on the table "… board."

Peter shrugged, rather more calmly than I would have done in his situation.

"This job," I asked. "Is it legal?

He looked at me strangely for a moment: "Yes," he said, scratching his beard and looking out of a porthole. "The illegal bit was done years ago, but you'll find out about that soon enough. Now; let's get this old girl moving!"

"Where are we going?" asked Peter.

"Norfolk," came the reply, simply enough.

"In for a penny …" I murmured. "Or half a crown."

We stowed our rucksacks under our berths and struggled out of the cabin in order to cast off.

"Just how do we get to Norfolk?" I called back as I unwound the stern line from a cleat on the pontoon.

O'Brien was already tinkering with the outboard but he looked up with a grin: "Seven miles north east of here we join the Great Ouse. That'll take us to King's Lynn. After that it's the Wash."

Peter, jumping aboard with the bow line, muttered something about hoping O'Brien knew what he was doing.

"I think he does," I said, as the engine roared into life, but I knew I was trying hard to convince the both of us. The Wash may look like a well sheltered bay on a map, but I'd read somewhere that its low-lying coasts meant it was seriously exposed to the weather. Then there were the notoriously shifting sands … and primary school memories concerning King John's baggage train foundering in the mud as the causeway crumbled … came surging back.

Samphire pulled away from the pontoon, checked slightly as the dinghy's towline snapped taut, and then picked up speed a little, settling on a steady four knots, which I guessed was probably both the limit of her power and the maximum allowed by British Waterways. O'Brien abandoned the tiller and spun the small wheel on the cabin bulkhead to correct our course. "An adaptation," he said proudly. "I can steer from here too. Better view for'ard. All done with wires and pulleys."

"But you went aft to start her up," I ventured.

"Ah yes," he replied. "I can *stop* the motor from here in emergencies, but I can't start it without the pull-cord. No battery, you see. It's an old British Seagull … quite a classic, really.

No wonder it sounded like my dad's BSA Road Rocket.

Then I remembered the sail: "It's an odd rig."

He nodded vigorously: "Indeed. She was bermudan originally, like most yachts, but she'd lost her boom and sails before I got her so I stepped the tabernacle further for'ard and had a standing lugs'l made. Much simpler, and she won't capsize in anything less than a force five … even with the centreboard up. That's under the saloon table, by the way."

(I thought I'd caught my knees on something when we were below!)

The cockpit was really little more than an open porch for the companionway into the cabin and it was unusually central to allow for a decked area aft; another strange feature in so small a boat. I wondered if it had originally been intended to house an inboard. O'Brien noticed my interest and explained that it was his own berth.

"Take a look," he said.

I bent down and opened a small cupboard-like door. Inside was a narrow slot with a sleeping bag on an airbed, lit only by a very small skylight which I suspected had once been an engine hatch. I could have sworn there was a whiff of diesel. The Seagull, of course, ran on petrol.

"I was using the saloon up till this morning," he said. "But you two obviously need that!"

"Rather you than me," I grunted. "Looks like a coffin."

"Okay at this time of year," he said. "But no space for a heater when it's cold."

I straightened up. The timbers which formed the berths in the saloon continued aft into the cockpit, providing benches to either side. They were narrower here, though, thus allowing more room to manoeuvre. A wooden box was screwed to the port bench, just below the wheel on the bulkhead. O'Brien opened it to reveal a beautiful old brass compass complete with concentric gimbals.

"I lock it below when *Samphire's* unattended of course," he said.

Of course.

Starboard of the companionway, a small brass clock and barometer were mounted on the bulkhead but , attractive as they were, I could see they were modern repros and it was probably safe to leave them, even when alongside a busy town quay somewhere like King's Lynn. I also noticed a small brass bell just inside the sliding doghouse and wondered if O'Brien actually rang the regulation half-hourly changes.

"Only for show," he said, anticipating my question. "I can never remember the damn sequence! Useful for waking the relief though, if we ever need to mount night watches."

The voyage down the drain was a little frustrating because the high floodbanks on either hand blocked out the view. Even after an hour or so we had little sense of having got anywhere. Mind you, the Fens are so flat and featureless that it probably would not have made any difference if we had been able to see them. At lunchtime we came to a place where Van Reuygen's Drain was crossed by another waterway and we had to pull in and work out how to open a swing bridge which carried its towpath across the main line. O'Brien didn't particularly

The Ditchcrawler

want to lower the mast in order to shoot the bridge. Happily, there was a waterside pub in the angle of the two drains – the very twin of the *Six Horseshoes* - but called the *Van Reuygen Arms*. The signboard, however, was missing so the precise nature of the good Dutchman's heraldic blazon remained a mystery.

We went ashore and acquired beer and sandwiches which we consumed under a faded sun umbrella in the garden near the water. Peter and I tried to coax O'Brien into telling us more about the job he had mentioned, but he was not to be drawn so we changed tack.

"What was the significance of the half crowns?" I asked.

"Nothing whatever," he said. "But obviously Mr Sherriff needed some form of identification before he pulled your pints and cooked your dinner. I just happened to have the coins so I sent them to you and told him what to expect."

"Why Bradwell St Helen?" asked Peter.

"Conveniently situated," O'Brien said. "Not too far from our destination and roughly equidistant between it and both your homes. And on my own route, of course."

"Your route from where?" I asked.

"Chester," he said. "That's where I live now."

"All this way by water? Must have taken forever!"

"Tell me about it! Canals mostly, at least to start with. Shropshire Union first … joined Trent-Mersey at Middlewich … followed the network down to Northampton via Brum … then out on the Nene to the Fen Drains like this."

"So how long in total?" I asked. "Time-wise?"

"Three weeks or so … to date."

I wasn't surprised, but something hit me which may have been floating around my subconscious for some time.

"Three weeks," I mused. "And possibly another two with us by the time we're done. That's five weeks to do as you please. You've got to be a teacher?"

"Logical but wrong!" he laughed."

"So what are you then?" asked Peter.

He did not answer for a moment, and then gave a typically evasive reply. "A man, as you are." It might have been a quotation, I thought.

"You know what he means," I said calmly but firmly, starting to take up cudgels on Pete's behalf.

"Yes but that's all I can say at the moment," he replied. "I suppose you *could* say I'm unemployed, though."

"So how can you possibly employ *me*?" snapped Pete, the exasperation starting show at last.

O'Brien coloured.

"A fair question," he acknowledged. "But trust me. There's a way through this."

"And another thing," said Pete, the bit firmly between his teeth now. "You've got a fair sized boat here and you can afford to pay other peoples' bills. On the dole? It just doesn't add up."

O'Brien finished his beer and picked the last crumbs out of his beard and ate them.

"All right," he said at last. "I'll come clean. I left Cardiff because I was fed up with endless Court Reports about minor traffic offences and so on." (I nodded in sympathy: it's every journalist's right of passage.) "I tried freelancing, but every editor I sent anything sent it back and said I should give up journalism and try fiction. So I did."

"Successfully?" I asked.

"Just the one. Historical novel."

"Did it sell?" asked Pete, genuinely impressed, I think.

"Just enough copies to pay for *Samphire* – I'd always fancied a boat by the way - and a few extras … like your bill at the *Three Horseshoes*."

I shook my head in reasonably good-humoured disbelief as we got up and returned to the boat. O'Brien went ahead to check the contents of the dinghy – whatever they were – and I put my hand on Peter's arm.

"Have you ever read *The Riddle of the Sands?*" I asked. He shook his head. "It's about this bloke who gets a telegram from a slight acquaintance telling him to drop everything, go to Denmark and meet up with him on his yacht. Then they sail to the Friesian Islands for reasons which are by no means clear, get entangled with German spies and eventually realise they're the only Brits who can warn the government that what we now call World War One is about to break out. Doesn't that all sound rather familiar?"

"What? You mean O'Brien's lined us up for World War Three?" he said with a painful smile.

I forced a laugh as we climbed aboard again.

*

At about four o'clock we reached Flitterby Sluice, where Van Reuygen's Drain cuts through the west bank of the Great Ouse in order to join it at a sharp angle. We tied up on a pontoon in the transit basin and began to recce the junction on foot. The Ouse at this point is still tidal, so the lock was necessarily more complicated than most, with counter-directional gates to allow for reverse flow on the high springs … to say nothing of assorted relief channels to cope with excess water coming from almost any direction. For me it was a somewhat daunting prospect but O'Brien appeared to remain calm and collected. The trouble was, though, you never knew what he was really thinking.

Clearly we would have to take our position in a queue of boats wishing to lock out when the keepers deemed it safe to do so.

We climbed up onto a concrete viewing platform by the big dams and sluices.

"Still flooding," he said, looking down at the turgid, muddy flow.

"The water's coming inland faster than we could make against it. We'll have wait till the slack. Er … that's the turn of the tide." He produced a well thumbed tide table from his pocket and examined it carefully. "High water here at 23.06 tonight, but I don't suppose they'll open the gates for us at that time. Next one's 11.36 tomorrow morning, but they'll probably open up about ten. The flow will have slowed considerably by then."

And so we spent our first night aboard *Samphire* in the safety of the transit pool.

At the for'ard end of the saloon a hatch opened into a tiny, triangular forepeak containing a miniature camping stove, but O'Brien had rummaged under the tarp over the dinghy and produced a larger model with two burners and a rather more capacious gas cylinder. He set this up in the well of the cockpit and proceeded to cook up a mixture of baked beans, frankfurters and sweet corn, culled from the five week supply which we discovered was stored in every available nook and cranny - including the dinghy - along with assorted nautical bits and pieces.

We sat up until well after dark, Peter on the port bench with O'Brien to starboard. I perched on the lip of the after deck with my legs dangling either side of the hatchway into O'Brien's berth. He'd produced a bottle Bushmills from somewhere, which we drank out of our tin mugs once the coffee was finished. It was still warm and we were aware of other sailors enjoying the stillness. Snatches of conversation, bursts of companionable laughter and the chink of glasses echoed over the basin. Some had gone ashore to light proper barbecues, and feathers of blue-grey smoke drifted under the pink sky. Probably thanks to the Bushmills, we were pretty companionable aboard *Samphire* too, despite the weirdness of the situation. Even Pete, who had the most to loose, was mellowing noticeably.

"My uncle Jim had an old boat once," he said. "Kept her at Lytham St Anne's."

"Oh yes? What sort?" O'Brien asked.

Pete screwed up his eyes as he tried to remember: "Something local to the region, as I recall."

"Morecambe Bay Prawner? Otherwise known as a Nobby?"

"That's it!" said Pete. "But he couldn't afford to keep it for long. He had this saying: *A boat is a hole in the water into which you constantly pour money!*"

"Very true!" O'Brien laughed. "*Samphire* here is just about as big a hole as my royalties permit."

"This novel of yours," I asked. "What's it about?"

O'Brien took a slow sip of his whisky and said he'd give us a copy each to read at our leisure, but we both demanded an oral synopsis. Eventually he gave in.

"Okay. Well … it's about Norfolk's answer to Robin Hood; a fourteenth century outlaw called Watkyn de Snettisham."

"A true story?" asked Pete.

"Perhaps. Like Robin Hood, he's a mixture of history, myth and legend. I hope what I've done is produce an imaginative but credible account of what may really have happened."

"And what was that?" I asked.

O'Brien paused for another slurp.

"I've only been to Norfolk once before," he continued. "When I was a kid. Sixteen or so. With my parents. We were camping at a place called Skolme, on the coast. It was then I first heard about *Old Snetty* … as he's popularly known. Very much a local Norfolk legend, you see. He was never as famous as Robin Hood … though some of the stories about them are virtually identical. Anyway, it seems he was a yeoman living in the reign of Richard II."

"Yeoman?" asked Pete.

"Higher than a serf. A free peasant with a few strips of land to call his own. A yeoman could be quite prosperous actually, a bit like the Russian Kulaks, I suppose. Minor gentry, even. However, there would have been several feudal layers between him and the nobility proper, so - come the new poll tax in 1381 – his land holdings probably got squeezed and he felt the pinch like almost everyone else."

Something clicked for me: "Ah … the Peasants' Revolt!"

"Exactly. The story goes that when the rising spread into East Anglia, de Snettisham played a leading part in its organisation … almost the *Wat Tyler* of Norfolk, in fact. He raised the banner of St George at

Docking and recruits flocked to his side by the hundred. They even managed to occupy Norwich for a while, before heading back west to link up with other rebels out here in the Fens. But by this time things were going wrong further south. After some initial success, the Kent and Essex rebels started fighting among themselves over whether or not to accept the King's concessions; Tyler was killed of course, and things fell apart. Some fought, some fled, and poor old Watkyn was left with a moderately sized army up in Norfolk and nothing to do with it. Apparently he tried to persuade them to disband but they wouldn't hear of it and decided to make a second attempt on Norwich. As a man of honour, he couldn't possibly abandon them and was thus obliged to march with them to their doom."

"So what happened?" I asked eagerly. He had us both enthralled now.

"The Bishop of Norwich happened," he said grimly. "Henry le Despenser was back in town with an army of his own. Bishops did that kind of thing in those days, believe it or not. Anyway, they headed out to intercept Old Snetty's force and caught up with him near North Walsham. It was an unequal fight from the beginning ... what with the Bishop's cronies on horseback in full armour ... no doubt seeing it all as a jolly old hunting expedition. Snetty's archers took their toll, but sheer weight of numbers pushed them back into a wood where a party of dismounted knights - who'd already outflanked them - cut them to pieces amongst the trees. One version has it that some of the rebels fled into North Walsham and made a heroic last stand in the churchyard."

"And Old Snetty himself?"

"Disappeared. But that's where the legends begin."

"*Diflanniad*", I said under my breath.

"What?"

"*Diflanniad.*" It's Welsh. It means to vanish mysteriously. Like Owen Glyndwr."

"Just like Old Snetty," O'Brien agreed. "Officially he was never seen alive again, and the Bishop even produced a mutilated corpse purporting to be his. But few believed it. Soon there were reported sightings of a bloodied and shambling figure lurking in the remoter parts of Norfolk … but particularly over towards the Wash. That's where Snettisham is, by the way. Just north of King's Lynn. Also the saltmarshes further north still.

"Soon he was joined by other remnants and they became guerrillas … or bandits … depending on your point of view."

"Don't tell me …" Pete interjected. "Robbing the rich and giving to the poor?"

"More or less," O'Brien replied. "As I say, his stories are very similar to Robin Hood's. Anyway, his fame lived on but only in East Anglia. I've even read that country folk were still putting food out for *Old Snetty* and his merry men well into living memory, would you believe!"

Actually, I could. Folklore is a very powerful thing.

"Do people still claim to see him?" asked Pete.

"Oh yes," replied O'Brien. "Sometimes with Black Shuck on a lead."

"Black what?"

"Black *Shuck*. Norfolk's *other* legend. A giant black dog with burning red eyes and phosphorescent foam around its mouth."

All three of us laughed, but not entirely with mirth, I think.

"These saltmarshes," I asked. "How extensive are they?"

He ducked into the saloon for a moment and emerged with an Ordnance Survey map and a torch. We really were losing the light now. Spreading the map on the coachroof he used the torch to illuminate the northeastern extremity of the Wash.

"From Hunswick," he said. "The *corner* of Norfolk if you like … eastwards at least as far as Wakeney. Thirty miles or so. "

I took the torch and examined the stretch of north-facing coastline he had indicated: a long belt of saltmarsh, mudflats and dunes, threaded through with a complicated array of channels, creeks and lagoons. Some of the wider inlets boasted villages … or at least hamlets. Skolme; Turnham Staithe; Stitchwell; Chesterfleet and Boverey Staithe. By contrast, Cokeham Pumps and Wakeney looked as if they might even be small towns with proper harbours. East of Wakeney there was a place called Flatte – appropriately - but here the marshland gave way to shingle and the coastline started to curve gently south towards Sherringham and Cromer.

"It's a difficult place to describe, really," said O'Brien, clearly recalling his teenage ramblings around Skolme. "Popular with small boat sailors and ornithologists, but not yet inundated with tourists. There are good beaches on the seaward side of the marshes, but you have to walk miles to reach them on causeways which can easily flood. And it's a hell of a way to carry the hamper and the deckchairs! Much better to arrive by boat."

"The villages," said Peter. What are they like?"

"Picturesque. Brick and flint cottages; windmills; curiously vast churches; ramshackle boat sheds ... oh, and some excellent pubs."

"Where exactly are we going?" I asked.

I sensed his guard returning.

"Oh ... somewhere round about Skolme or Turnham Staithe, maybe. Or Stitchwell, perhaps. Come on lads; we'd best turn in! It's late. No need to set watches in still water. Oh by the way ... if you need the loo, I'm afraid it's a case of *bucket and chuck it* ... but don't actually chuck it until we're on tidal water tomorrow!" He indicated a zinc pail under one of the side benches.

He did a quick inspection of the deck tackle, folded the map and opened the door to his berth. We bade him goodnight and squeezed into the saloon. Sleeping bags were laid out on the padded benches now, but getting undressed and into them required an awkward degree of bodily contortion. However, once abed it was comfortable enough.

Just before I dropped off, Pete whispered an observation.

"You know what's *really* odd about all this?"

"Tell me."

"It's as if Mike's researching the background to his book *after* he's written it. You'd think he'd have made this trip years ago. So why now? And why us?"

"I suppose we'll find out," I yawned.

"Perhaps that's what worries me," he said. "Goodnight."

"Goodnight."

I *think* I slept well … despite a dream about an armoured bishop in a steel mitre chasing a huge black dog with burning eyes.

THREE

The following morning, Monday, the tide had slackened sufficiently by just after 10.00 to allow for a transit. So we followed a line of three cruisers and a brightly painted narrowboat through the complicated sequence of gates and basins which – fortunately – were manned by British Waterways officials. All we had to do was follow their shouted instructions and eventually nose out into the coffee-coloured, esturine waters of the Great Ouse. The flood was still coming in, but slowly now, and we were able to swing our bows to port and make headway against it.

The narrowboat turned to starboard and went with the weakening flow, doubtless anxious to gain access to another still water canal before the tide turned again. The three cruisers must have had pretty powerful engines because they surged to port ahead of us and disappeared round a bend within minutes of leaving the lock.

By mid-day we were able to cut back on the revs and haul up the sail. We had the ebb with us now and a light wind on the port quarter pushed us along nicely. The dinghy, however, was bouncing around all over the place and threatened to bump the prop. We hauled it alongside and made fast. This complicated the steering but O'Brien seemed to get the hang of it easily enough.

"Have you done any tidal sailing before?" I asked.

"No," he replied cheerfully. "But I've read all the right books!"

Pete and I glanced at each other with raised eyebrows. Coming from Lancaster, Peter would know all about tidal rivers … even if he had never actually tried sailing on Morecambe Bay or the Lune in his uncle's Nobby.

As the ebb strengthened I began to worry that we would loose steerage way – the current moving faster than the boat – but the breeze picked up as well and we retained control. O'Brien put me in charge of the rig as I'd done some sailing before. It was a pleasure: a standing lugs'l more or less looks after itself and I just tensioned or slackened the sheet as required; sometimes making it off on a cleat but more usually keeping hold of it so I could actually feel the sail drawing us north towards the Wash.

Somehow we reached King's Lynn, where the river became very wide; a quarter of a mile, perhaps, if you included its muddy margins. Then, once through the bypass bridge, we encountered a new potential hazard: ships. Big ones … at least by local standards. Dutch and German coasters mostly, lining the quays on the right bank. It was approaching low water now and most of them were obviously sitting on the mud, tilting drunkenly towards the cranes and hoppers or leaning shyly away from the slimy wall. We took advantage of our shallow draught to get past them and carry on towards the sea, keeping to the middle with the centre board up just in case. The town sprawled along the right bank; tall warehouses, Dutch gables and pantiled roofs aplenty … as well as all the detritus of an active, working port: stacks of sawn timber; rolls of sheet steel and pyramids of sacks of agri-chemicals of one sort or another.

O'Brien dithered about stopping for fuel but eventually decided we had enough in the dinghy. I was mildly disappointed. Lynn looked like an interesting place – an old Hanseatic town if I remembered correctly – which might repay a visit. Some other time, maybe.

At last we could see the mouth of the Ouse and a proper marine horizon beyond. Perspective made the high floodbanks taper towards each other but this was countered by the actual widening of the river, the scale of which was emphasised by the pair of immense pylons carrying power lines over the water, high enough, it seemed, for the tallest of tall ships to pass underneath. Below the lines and between the pylons was the sea, a rich, shimmering cobolt blue in the summer sun.

"Life jacket time," called O'Brien, handing the wheel to Pete while he rummaged in his berth once more, pulling out three ancient flotation aids of canvas and kapok. "To be worn at all times once we're at sea."

They stank of mildew and brine, and would doubtless make getting in and out of the saloon even more of an acrobatic exercise, but we struggled into them nonetheless.

To my huge relief, O'Brien also produced a proper admiralty chart and taped it to the doghouse lid. Ordnance Survey maps are good … but they don't mark much in the way of seabed features, maritime hazards or prevailing currents.

"I thought the Wash was supposed to be a bay," said Pete as we slipped past the beacons marking the extremities of the floodbanks and into open water.

"It is," said O'Brien. "But the surrounding country is mostly below sea level so you can't see it. Just the levees … if you're lucky."

"It's at least as big as Morecambe Bay," I added, appealing to Pete's local knowledge. "But without the mountains!"

But we could, of course, see land to starboard as we worked our way northwards along Norfolk's west coast. Low, wooded hills undulated behind a beach of mud and shingle. There were open patches of heath where purple drifts of heather blended with bright bracken just about to turn coppery.

"Mostly part of the Sandringham estate," said O'Brien. "Snettisham's over there too."

Peter was sent to the foredeck with instructions to keep a strict lookout for sand banks or anything else which might impede our progress. "Especially lobster pot buoys … the ones with flags on. See anything you're not happy about, give us a shout and point in the direction you think we should steer."

I looked at the chart: we were following a marked channel known as the Cork Hole, between the sand bars of Styleman's Middle to port and Ferrier's Sand to starboard. They were still submerged, but there was definitely breaking foam on the surface, which gave us a pretty good idea of where they were. The weather was perfect; cloudless and bright, but breezy enough to spank us along at a reasonable clip. We had let the dinghy out to the end of her line again and she bobbed along happily in our wake. We even risked putting the centreboard down to help with the steering.

O'Brien pointed over our starboard bow: "*Hunzick* cliffs coming into view," he said, using the local pronunciation for Hunswick. "The only true cliffs in the whole of East Anglia!"

"I thought they had cliffs at Cromer?" I replied, recalling one of my grandmother's many jigsaw puzzles.

"So they'll tell you," he laughed. "But they're just big clay bluffs down there. These are the real thing. Take a look through your binoculars."

I raised my glasses and brought them into focus. The land had been rising gently as the trees gave way to buildings but it came to an abrupt end, forming a clear vertical drop to the dunes just north of the town. A stubby white lighthouse crowned the summit. The really remarkable thing, though, was the colouration of the cliffs.

"They're striped!" I said. "Like a layer cake."

Apparently they are unique: layers of red and white chalk sitting on a band of very local rust-coloured carr stone … the only *real* rock in East Anglia, according to O'Brien.

"For someone who's only been to Norfolk once you're phenomenally well informed!" I cried over the rising breeze.

"Research for my book," he retorted cheerfully.

I glanced up at the sun and then at my watch. The afternoon was well advanced and I wondered if we were going to anchor or put in somewhere for the night … or carry on round the end of the cliffs to St Fursey's Point and the North Sea proper. The latter was a somewhat alarming prospect. Certainly the chart indicated a plethora of light-buoys and floats which doubtless rendered night navigation possible, but I seriously doubted there was anyone aboard who could interpret them correctly.

O'Brien seemed to read my mind; not for the first time.

"We'll stop at Hunzick," he said.

"But there's no harbour!" I replied, gesturing towards the chart.

"Don't worry. We'll run her up the beach. She takes the ground happily enough."

The chart did indicate some kind of channel – or at least a vague depression in the seabed – pointing inland just north of South Sunk Sand. Finding it might have been problematic as it was totally un-buoyed, but eventually Peter spotted what looked like a slightly darker patch of water roughly in line with the stubby pier. I don't think we ever found out if it really was the channel but we decided to risk it with the centreboard up. I sheeted out the sail just about as far as it would go as we turned stern-on to the wind. It bellied and snapped for a moment before filling more like a Viking squares'l and we ran in straight towards the pier, finally grounding within a hundred yards of the storm ravaged and incomplete piece of seaside Victoriana. (We didn't know, of course, but what was left of it was destined to go the way of all flesh before the coming winter was out.)

The tide was falling swiftly now and, on O'Brien's instructions, we splashed through the shallows carrying an anchor up the beach towards the town, burying it in the firmest patch of sand we could find. Later, when the tide had retreated still further, we ran out a smaller anchor astern and thrust it firmly into an exposed seam of glutinous clay. Being virtually flat bottomed, *Samphire* sat comfortably enough on the gleaming wet sand.

It was tempting to run ashore and find a pub, but O'Brien was concerned about vandalism. Hunswick was a fairly genteel little town, but its funfair and arcades did bring in a rowdier element from some of the Midland cities … or so the locals complained.

This time we set up the stove and the stools on the beach once it was dry enough. More beans and sausages, of course. And coffee. And Bushmills. I was beginning to wonder if there were any alternatives stashed in the dinghy … but at least there was bacon for breakfast. Peter whispered something about the effect of the baked beans on the atmosphere in our sleeping quarters, but I pointed out that the mouldy stench of the ancient life jackets would more than compensate.

When we had eaten, we set night watches for the first time: ten to twelve; twelve to three and three to six. This was not for fear of the tide. We were safe enough for the time of year and O'Brien was confident that the anchors would hold if the sea returned. He was far more concerned about late night revellers. Personally, I felt we were far enough away from the prom not to attract attention. After all, we were showing no riding lights as we were not actually afloat .

Once again it was a delightfully warm evening and we sat up late, relaxing with our coffee and Irish. There was music coming from somewhere; the funfair, probably. Quietly at first … strengthening as the sun went down. Country and Western seemed to predominate and something I vaguely recognised drifted towards us over the sand. Two or three female voices harmonising wistfully about the Mississippi, yet steadily underpinned with a solid beat. I found myself tapping a foot on the sand.

"Look!" said Pete, suddenly pointing seawards. "That can't be right!"

Following his gaze I saw nothing amiss. "What can't?"

"This *is* the East Coast, right?"

"Sure."

"So why is the sun setting over there?'

He was right. The flaming orb of the dying sun was plunging towards the horizon in the wrong place entirely.

O'Brien laughed: "Hunzic's *other* claim to fame, after the stripy cliffs! The only East Coast resort facing west. That's the Wash remember, so the sun both rises and sets over the sea."

Peter winced and almost physically kicked himself. He was supposed to be a geographer after all. "Of course! Stupid of me."

I vaguely remembered an old girlfriend from Yorkshire telling me something similar about Whitby, but perhaps that was only at certain times of the year, so I held my council. When the sun finally did disappear I noticed a faint bloom of light on the horizon which didn't seem to relate to the afterglow. Wrong colours.

O'Brien read my mind again.

"Skegness," he said. "Lincolnshire. If we were up on the cliffs you'd see the Big Dippers and the Ferris Wheel, all lit up of course. Down here they're hidden by the curvature of the Earth,"

"So it *is* round, after all," Peter joked.

With that settled, we packed away the gear and turned in. I took the first watch, catnapping in the cockpit and occasionally jumping overboard and pacing the beach to keep awake. At midnight I went below and shook Peter. The brass bell wasn't necessary.

*

The rest of the night was uneventful, but when dawn broke on Tuesday, the tide seemed even further out than it had been the evening before. O'Brien frowned and flicked through his tide table. I sensed – for the first time – that he had miscalculated something.

"Does it include Hunswick?" I asked.

"Should do," he said. "It's based on Boston and King's Lynn. It was fine on the Ouse."

"Well that explains it," put in Pete, having seemingly recovered his geographical know-how. *Physical* geographers probably made a study of tides, I supposed. He continued, warming to his theme like the expert he doubtless was: "Tides are consistent, but not constant. High and low water each normally occur twice every twenty-four hours, but advancing by half an hour every twelve hours … as we saw at Flitterby Sluice. The varying range I'm sure you both know about – big *springs* at full moon and new moon – but with a much more limited range in between … called *neap tides*. It all gets exaggerated around an equinox, of course. Next month, in our case.

"What people forget, though, is that the pattern also cycles up and down rivers and along the coast. So – for example – high tide at London Bridge will be later than at, say, Deptford which in turn will be much later than Whitstable. And so on. Out here I should think the ebb from the Fen rivers will be seriously modified by a tidal stream coming down the North Sea. You need a more local table, Mike."

We both gaped at him. It was the longest speech we'd ever heard him make.

"Well," said O'Brien at last. "It looks like we've got plenty of time to kill so you'd best run ashore and get one. I don't think there's a proper chandlery here so try the Tourist Information. It's on the corner of the Town Green. Top left. Can't miss it."

"I'll come too," I said quickly. "I fancy some fresh bread and cheese. And fruit. Don't want scurvy, now, do we?"

O'Brien assented readily enough, so Pete and I strode off up the slope of the beach past the pier whose skeletal limbs were festooned with mussels and dripping seaweed.

"Quite a speech!" I said, once we were out of earshot of the boat.

"Sorry. I was overcompensating for last night's gaff about the sunset."

"Thought you might be!"

" I've had a thought," he said after a minute or two. "You've done a bit of sailing, I gather?"

"A bit. Dinghies only though, on lakes and ponds. Not much sea where I come from!"

"And I know about tides and so on. Mike seems fairly competent regarding *Samphire*, but he's as good as admitted it's all pretty much new to him. Do you think he chose us because he needs us? You for canvas and ropes and things and me for navigation? He's not mentioned it, but I *can* read a compass."

"Even if you can't tell east from west … sorry, that was cruel!"

He shrugged it off.

"But that's the point!" he said. "I wasn't *looking* at a compass last night, was I? I just made a daft assumption."

"As we all do," I replied hastily. "Don't worry about it. And yes, I suppose he might think he needs us, but why choose to travel by boat at all? Why not just drive down to Norfolk and save himself three weeks?"

"Perhaps he doesn't drive."

By now we had reached the concrete steps up to the promenade. From here the Town Green sloped gently on upwards towards the diminutive town centre. A very gothic hotel in the ubiquitous brown carr stone loomed to our left and I could just make out a Tourist Information sign on the front of a similar but smaller building beyond it. We walked diagonally across the Green, where fat gulls pecked ferociously at scraps of yesterday's discarded fish suppers, quite oblivious to our presence. The information office, it transpired, did not open until ten, so we decided to look for a bakery and a greengrocer. In the event, we made do with a small supermarket next to a substantial novelty shop festooned with straw sunhats, colourful towels and the kind of inflatable beach toys calculated to give the Coastguard Service apoplexy. We still had ten minutes to kill so we wondered over to the hotel and found a plaque informing the world that the *Golden Griffin* was the first (and for some years the *only*) building in *New* Hunswick. I wondered where *Old* Hunswick had been and if there were still any discernable trace of it.

"They'll tell you in the info. place," said Peter, logically enough, and even as he spoke a key rattled next door, a burglar alarm control box bleeped for a moment and the Tourist Office was open for business.

A helpful lady of a certain age sold me two tide tables; one for Skegness and one for Cokeham Pumps. "We're about half way between them here," she said. "So just split the difference on the times."

I glanced at Pete for confirmation that this would work and he nodded gently.

Moments later we were heading back across the Green with our purchases. The sun was well up now and the sea – clearly on its way back - sparkled in a morning haze. Bathers and even surfers were striding over the sand in growing numbers … not that there was any surf to speak of. *Samphire* sat on the sand near the crumbing pier like an insect basking in the heat.

Using the tide tables in the manner prescribed by the lady in the Tourist Information office, O'Brien concluded that there would be enough water to float *Samphire* sometime between twelve and one, and Pete was in broad agreement that this was likely. We took in the stern anchor but left the best bower in place for the time being. Then we dragged the dinghy out to the end of her cable, which was roughly where the stern anchor had been: once she was floating we'd know it was only a matter of minutes before *Samphire* herself would start to lift.

I made bread and cheese sandwiches so we could enjoy a light lunch while we waited. O'Brien produced a pot of tea from below, presumably having used the small stove in the forepeak. I'd picked up a glossy leaflet in the tourist office and skim-read it between mouthfuls. It transpired that there was indeed an *Old* Hunswick: the original village, which was tucked away in the woods about a mile inland. *New* Hunswick – or simply *Hunzick* as everyone called it – was an entirely Victorian confection, having been the pet project of the very wealthy squire whose land it stood on. He'd literally built his own seaside resort at the bottom of his garden. Nice!

By 12:30 the dinghy was floating and ten minutes later so were we. Peter and I hauled in the anchor and jumped overboard while the water was still only thigh deep. We manoeuvred her round to face the sea as O'Brien started the motor. We hauled ourselves back on board as Samphire headed out past the dinghy which flipped round to follow us when the line snapped taught.

The breeze was still coming out of the south west and I soon had the sail back up and drawing nicely. There was a slight swell running now, and we'd taken on a mild corkscrew roll … the kind of motion which is almost bound to make landlubbers feel a bit queasy. But nobody complained or looked green about the gills.

Soon we were level with the north end of the banded cliffs, which suddenly gave way to dunes and saltmarsh. St Fursey's point (where an Irish missionary had allegedly come ashore to convert the pagan Angles) was really just a sand spit curling protectively around a marshy lagoon. We eased north a touch in order to clear any hidden banks but pulled back in a little at Skolme. Here the rampart of dunes completely obscured the marshes behind them where, according to O'Brien, there was a famous bird reserve.

Low hills were just visible above the dazzlingly white dunes, with more open pasture and fewer woods than we'd seen south of Hunswick.

"The Lingstead Downs," said O'Brien. "Chalky. Not very high, but worth exploring on foot."

"Didn't you say you'd camped around here?" I asked.

"Yes. Skolme village. We'll see it in a minute."

Sure enough, a gap opened in the dunes to reveal the saltmarsh. I glanced at the chart to see if there was an approach to the village, but it didn't look like it.

"Silted up years ago," said O'Brien. "Before my time. But all these little villages were busy ports once … a century ago at least. We can get into the next one, though."

I looked at the chart again. "Turnham Staithe?"

He nodded. "It's a very narrow entrance but I think there'll be enough water in the Gut by the time we get there. We can always anchor off and move in later I we need to."

"Gut?"

"The creek leading up to the village. There are some old jetties we can tie up on if we're lucky."

I glanced back towards Skolme and just spotted a squat church tower and some red pantiled roofs. They were gone as soon as I saw them … elusive, like the rare birds which haunted these lonely places.

In the event, there was just about enough water in Turnham Gut for us to put our nose into the creek and sniff our way in, so to speak. O'Brien fired up the motor and I dropped the sail. It was a fairly tortuous passage, zig-zagging between muddy shoals and the barnacled ribs of old wrecks. Sometimes the towering banks of sedge closed in on both sides and brushed along our gunwales, their feathery pods showering us with seed as we passed beneath. That was when we discovered that Pete was a martyr to hay fever. Once the dinghy snagged on something and brought us up short but we managed to pull her free.

This was real *ditchcrawling*, as they say in these parts.

Actually, the tide was following us in and the channel was paradoxically deepening the further inland we got. Suddenly it widened and we saw the rickety jetties lining the bank to starboard. A few were occupied with grubby-looking shellfish boats which may or may not have seen any service in the last decade or so. Most, however, were untenanted and we nudged up against one of the more serviceable examples, our timbers squelching on the ancient tyres festooned along the front of the dock.

"Keep the lines loose," O'Brien advised. "It's not a floating pontoon, remember, and the tide's still rising."

It was a lonely spot – some might say bleak – with its rotting jetties and the whispering sedge. A ramshackle barn which served no obvious purpose stood on the right bank a few yards ahead of us and, further up still, something which may have been the base of a windmill lay crumbling into a choking mass of hawthorn and brambles. Oystercatchers skittered over the mud and curlews whauped mournfully as they streaked low over the marsh. Somewhere a dog was barking.

Black Shuck?

"But where's the village?" asked Peter.

"We're too low down," O'Brien replied. "You'll see it from the jetty."

And so we braved the once vertical (but by now seriously buckled and rusty iron ladder) up to the slimy grey planking which creaked ominously as we stepped onto it. O'Brien pointed inland and sure enough, beyond the quivering banks of sedge on the other side of the creek, we saw another squat church tower and the ubiquitous cluster of pantiled roofs.

"Small, then," remarked Pete.

"Yes. But it's got the *Sloop Inn*. Best pub in England! I'll treat you later."

It occurred to me that if we were all going to have a run ashore at the same time, we really ought to pay some attention to our mooring lines. O'Brien was right to leave them loose, but I reckoned we could devise a system of running knots and bights which would cater for both the ebb and the flow. When I suggested this, he just told me to get on with it. So I did. All being well, my improvisation would allow *Samphire* to rise and fall without drifting away from the jetty or capsizing on top of it: I wasn't entirely certain how sure-footed any of us would be when we returned from our night at the *Sloop!*

We didn't bother cooking. O'Brien assured us that the pub would meet all our culinary needs that evening, and once we were in striking distance of opening time we battened down the hatches and squelched over the wet ground to the rutted lane which led up to the village.

"It can't have rained, surely?" said O'Brien, splashing through a flooded pothole.

"No," said Pete. "The last tide must have been a hell of a big one. I know the equinox is a month away yet, but they can start to build early. We may have to do a bit of wading on the way back!"

He was right. The ground on either side of the road was riddled with shimmering, interconnected pools. I was struck by the vivid green of the low, springy vegetation between them and bent to look more closely.

"*Samphire*," called our host. "Like the boat. Boil it for a few seconds and serve with butter. *Poor man's asparagus* they call it round here, but much tastier in my opinion. Locally pronounced *sampha*, by the way. Remind me to gather some before we leave."

I chuckled to myself, remembering that I'd forgotten to ask him about the name.

We passed the old barn and the remains of the mill and came to a T junction. Turning left, the ancient smugglers' inn hove into view before us on the right. Steep, cream-rendered gables and tall chimneys rose above low, thick walls with small windows. Two jutting porches were almost lost in wreaths of flowering creeper and a fair number of drinkers sat outside at wooden tables. It was a very English idyll and I was amused that a seemingly professional Irishman should be so taken with it.

It isn't my brief to write an East Anglian pub guide here, but *not* to include a detailed description of the *Sloop Inn* would be to deprive the reader of a glorious fragment of social and local history. Whereas the *Six Horseshoes* had been a plain brick box, this was a rambling sprawl of architectural accretion. Innumerable snugs, bars and lounges sprouted and conjoined organically, each with its own unique floor level and degree (or lack!) of headroom. There were fireplaces everywhere, from cavernous inglenooks to ancient bread ovens built into walls. All the ceilings were heavily beamed and the spaces between the joists were hung with ancient tankards and jugs in pewter or brass, while the walls were heavy with farming implements and fishing tackle. Oars and harpoons were stacked in corners; shotguns, muskets and cutlasses graced the chimney breasts. There were pictures too: primitive *Pier Head* paintings of fishing boats and coasters … and sepia photos of village life a century ago.

Most surprising of all, however , was that the main lighting was provided by real, un-electrified paraffin lamps! These were being lit by a waiter as we walked in. It may still have been bright and sunny outside, but the *Sloop's* windows were so small and set in such deep embrasures that it was already dusk within. Soon the place smelt like the kind of hardware store I remembered from childhood.

Being August, it was of course busy with visitors and locals alike, but we found a table in a tiny but unoccupied snug where Pete and I sat down. O'Brien announced he was getting the drinks in and disappeared without asking what we wanted. He left a leather document case on the table which – oddly – I had no recollection of seeing as we'd walked up the lane. I suppose I'd been too preoccupied with the landscape as usual.

He returned with three pewter tankards. *Real* pewter: ie mostly lead, and a couple of centuries old at least.

"Hedgely's Old Scatterbrain!" he announced triumphantly. "Straight from the wood. None of your namby pamby pumps or taps here!"

We each took a pull at our pints and agreed it was pretty good stuff.

"Now," he said, slapping a hand on the document case. "To business. It's about time you found out a little more about this enterprise of ours, I think."

"Too right!" said Peter with feeling.

O'Brien unzipped the case and slid out a number of clear plastic wallets containing what looked like newspaper clippings.

"Well now," he began, but paused abruptly when a waiter appeared and handed us a menu each. "I don't think I told you exactly how I came to hear about Old Snetty, did I?

"When you were camping with your parents?" I asked.

"That's right, yes. We were on a farm near Skolme, that village we saw from the boat this afternoon. Mum, Dad and Sheila – that's my sister – spent most of their time on the beach. They didn't mind struggling through the marsh with all the gear, but I went exploring on my own most days. Up and down the coast and further inland a bit … into those hills I mentioned."

"The Lingstead Downs?"

"Yeah. There's a pub in Lingstead village called the *Rogue Unhung*. I couldn't resist going in to ask what it meant … and sample the beer of course!"

"Just *how* old were you then?" asked Pete.

"Sixteen. But I looked older: Long hair too. I made a very passable hippy, so I did! Or else they knew the local peeler was on holiday or something. Anyway, they served me a decent pint and the story of Watkyn de Snettisham to go with it."

"So what've you got there?" I asked, nodding at the bundle under his hand.

"See for yourself," he said, passing the plastic wallets across. I took the largest and Pete two smaller examples. Mine proved to contain the centre spread from a national tabloid and carried the headline: **FOLK HERO SAVES RAPE GIRL**. Peter's - one from the local rag and the other from the **TIMES** – were headlined **OLD SNETTY RESCUES DAMSEL IN DISTRESS** and **DISTURBING EVENTS IN NORFOLK VILLAGE** respectively. Each article dated from the end of the sixties.

I began to read:

Shocked residents of a quiet north Norfolk village learned last night how a pretty teenager was attacked and raped in broad daylight . The girl, whose name cannot be released for legal reasons, was walking along the normally peaceful back lane past a small wood near her home when a blue, open-topped sports car drew up and the driver offered her a lift. When she refused his offer, he got out and chased her into the trees where he committed the assault.

Then, according to the girl's own account, there was a noise in the bushes and a *wild, unkempt, red-headed figure*, dressed in rags and wielding some sort of *long axe or pike* jumped out shouting fiercely. The attacker ran back towards the road and the last thing she heard before passing out was the sound of a car starting. When she came round there was no sign of her rescuer. Despite severe shock, she managed to walk the half mile back to her home where her parents contacted the police immediately.

The people of Lingstead, just inland from the popular seaside town of Hunswick, now ask themselves whether the local legend of *Old Snetty* – Norfolk's answer to Robin Hood – could be true after all! Could Watkyn de Snettisham, the fourteenth century outlaw and

leader of the Common Man, have left his unmarked grave to protect the descendants of the people he'd once led against the infamous Bishop of Norwich in 1381?

Over the years there have been many stories of Old Snetty coming to the aid of distressed locals. In 1887, for example, a Stitchwell man ...

And so it went on, listing about eight sightings over the centuries. There was a photograph of the wood, and two artist's impressions: one of the attacker and one of Old Snetty; both based on the girl's descriptions.

The other two articles told the same story, but rather less sensationally ... even the one in the local rag. The *Times* pointed out (perhaps plausibly) that the victim, doubtless familiar with the legend, had possibly hallucinated whilst in shock. The *Coast Post* focussed on the blue sports car, suggesting that it might have been either a Triumph Spitfire or some make of MG. Were any such vehicles known in the locality?

Peter was the first to react, but just as he was drawing breath to speak, the waiter returned to take our orders. We settled on the Speciality of the Day, Stooky Blues in Champagne Sauce. (*Stooky Blues*, apparently, are unusually large cockles from just along the coast.)

"All very interesting," Peter continued. "But what's it got to do with us?"

O'Brien smiled that thin smile of his which gave nothing away.

"I propose," he said quietly. "To find Old Snetty."

We stared at him.

"What about the rapist? I asked.

He shook his head: "That's a job for the police. Mind you, they've had ten years to make an arrest with nothing to show for it yet."

"Was the car ever traced?" asked Pete.

"Not so far as I know."

Our food arrived and I turned my attention to the steaming bowl of Stooky Blues. There were finger bowls, too, with hot water and slices of lemon, and thick slices of crusty bread to mop up the sauce. Clearly this place had aspirations.

During the meal, O'Brien laid out his plans for the next couple of days.

When we eventually made our way – not *too* unsteadily – back to the boat, we discovered Peter had been right about the tide. It was lapping the edge of the lane and we did have to wade the last few yards to the jetty. *Samphire*, however, had risen comfortably up the poles and waited for us unscathed. It was gone midnight and the sky was a blaze of stars … more stars than sky, it seemed, and the Milky Way stood out like a crumpled strip kitchen foil unrolled across the heavens. We didn't bother setting watches. O'Brien dug out an old tin alarm clock and set it to wake him at the turn of the tide, so he could check all was well with our lines.

Once again I dreamed about the big dog with the burning eyes and the bishop in the steel mitre.

FOUR

So Wednesday morning found me on the bus back along the coast to King's Lynn, with a brief to dig up as much as I could about the rape story from the reference section of the town library. Mike and Peter were going to spend the day in the dinghy, footling about in the creeks with lead lines and compasses. I wasn't quite sue why, but it was an opportunity for Pete to show off his surveying skills I suppose. But I couldn't see how any of this related to O'Brien's claim that he was looking for Old Snetty. To be honest, though, when Michael had announced that intention I wasn't at all certain if he meant the elusive phantom or the presumably very human impersonator who had rescued the victim.

The route took in Snettisham and naturally I looked around from the top deck to see if there were any associations with the legend. There was nothing obvious: no *Old Snetty Tea Rooms or Outlaw's Arms*. In fact, judging by the intricately carved and brightly painted village sign - so typical of East Anglia - the good people of Snettisham identified more with the Ancient Britons, thanks to a major archaeological discovery in the area a few decades ago.

I found the library easily enough and was directed to the reference section where I was told that the twice-weekly *Coast Post* was available on microfilm should I require it, but the daily and county-wide *Anglian Courant* could be seen in bound hard copy. I opted for both and started at the microfilm reader while the big bound volumes were brought up from the basement and placed on a nearby table. Finding the article O'Brien had given Peter was easy because I already knew the date. I skim read it just to be sure that nothing vital had been lost in the fumes of last night's *Old Scatterbrain* and then scrolled on to the next edition. Here there was a progress report on the police investigation and an interview with the girl's parents. The investigation seemed to have been going nowhere and the interview was rather stilted ... I suppose because both the reporter and the parents were being careful to say nothing which would identify the victim by association. No easy task in somewhere as close knit as the north west corner of Norfolk.

The police had easily established that nobody within 45 miles of

Lingstead owned a blue MG or Triumph Spitfire; but conceded that there might be a few other makes of open topped sports car in the area and this was a line they were still pursuing. I rather got the impression that the local press was somewhat relieved at the failure to locate the vehicle, as this increased the chances that the rapist was an outsider. They were keen to help the police of course, but really didn't want to point the finger at someone known to half their readership. So much for cutting edge, investigative journalism!

Later editions relied on safer material, such as alleged sightings of Old Snetty within living memory. There was even a special letters column dedicated to readers' experiences or – more usually – the experiences of *friends of friends* of readers. Some of these were clearly very old stories which had simply mutated into current events the way these things do. Others were obviously made up by cranks, but a few had an air of sincerity about them, however unlikely the content. A woman walking her dog near Chesterfleet one evening claimed to have seen a whole army of ragged peasants with banners and pitchforks marching along the ridge of Salt Head Island, silhouetted coal black against a particularly dramatic sunset. It transpired that she was a retired history professor from Cambridge who'd specialised in fourteenth century popular unrest. Of course she'd known about the legend … but she'd also remained adamant that she had seen what she had seen.

Curiously, given O'Brien's story, I could only find one instance where the apparition had intervened directly in order to assist a living person. About three years earlier, a greengrocer's delivery driver had run out of petrol at a lonely spot between Wakeney and Flatte. Walking back towards Wakeney with a jerry can, he'd taken a short cut across the marsh and was stopped in his tracks by a dishevelled, tramp-like figure who assured him that if he returned to his van immediately all would be well. When he started to ask the tramp how he could possibly know, the figure just vanished … *"in a paaf o' smook"*. It was only then that it had occurred to the driver that he may have had a supernatural experience. He returned to his van and discovered – to his astonishment – that the tank was full.

I copied a few of these stories out long hand as I could hardly return to *Samphire* empty handed, but then turned my attention to the bound volumes of the *Anglian Courant*. There were two of them: 1893 to 1938 and 1939 to just a few years ago. Helpfully, each had a typewritten index pasted into the end papers. Naturally I started on the later volume as this would carry the main story. The earlier volume might prove useful for background later.

The *Courant* was a serious paper which was clearly meant to look like a national broadsheet. Its coverage of the Lingstead rape was carefully measured and less lurid that anything else I'd read. There were fewer ghost stories and more informed speculation as to the precise nature of the events of the here and now. The search for the blue sports car was deemed particularly important and there was less insistence that it must have been a Spitfire or an MG. Apparently a blue Austin Healey had been examined in Cromer and a Sunbeam Rapier in Norwich but, in both cases, the owners (and anyone else with access to these vehicles) had been able to produce unshakable alibis. Then the net had been extended as far as Peterborough to the west and Cambridge to the south. Here there was no shortage of blue sports cars, but with absolutely nothing to connect them or their owners with Lingstead.

Thanks to the index, I was able to jump swiftly from story to story without scanning every page. Then, despite the index, I suddenly found myself staring at a page which didn't seem to be carrying anything remotely relevant. It was full of land sales, stock prices and other agricultural matters. I quickly concluded that whoever had compiled the index had simply included it by accident. Easily done! I was just about to turn the page when I spotted a small paragraph down towards the bottom right hand corner:

Pregnancy Rumours

Maternity staff at King's Lynn General Hospital have refused to confirm or deny that their wing is currently looking after a number of women and girls who have recently fallen pregnant as a result of rape. The question arose out of an investigation by a Department of Health Select Committee into the welfare of rape victims generally, and of under age victims in particular . Of particular interest to the committee is the question of the efficacy of Maternity Wards over Specialist Homes and vice versa. A spokeswoman for the Maternity and Gynaecology Wards has said: "It is the policy of King's Lynn General Hospital never to discuss individual patients currently in our care. The findings of the Select Committee will doubtless be made public in due course."

I re-read it carefully and changed my mind about the compiler of the index. There was no mention of Old Snetty or Lingstead, but it was a story at least partly about rape. Coincidence? Possibly … but why include it in the index under the Old Snetty / Lingstead headings? Curiously, it was *not* indexed under *R* for *Rape*. I got the distinct impression that the compiler of the index was attempting to record something for posterity which he or she considered important without actually giving away any privileged information. If so, I was probably the first person to make the connection since the article had gone to press.

After that there was nothing more about the case until the following spring, when a stark headline appeared on a front page in late March: **LINGSTEAD TRAGEDY – THE FINAL ACT**.

I was totally unprepared for what followed.

The girl, now named as Julia Whitfield, had indeed fallen pregnant as a result of the rape, and – unusually even for that time – had died during childbirth. The child, believed to be a boy, had survived. I gulped involuntarily; it read like something from a Victorian novel. All manner of somewhat disjointed thoughts flittered through my head. How could this have happened in the Swinging Sixties? Had abortion not been an option? A question instantly followed by convulsive guilt on my part because there was nothing in the article to suggest that the child was in any way deformed or likely to be ill treated. And presumably there had been no indication that giving birth was likely to prove fatal for his mother. Nevertheless, the mere fact of the child's survival still conjured up sepia photographs of grubby workhouses and grim orphanages. Ridiculous, I know. Chances are it had been adopted by a loving family and was flourishing … by now getting ready for *big school* in a year or two. Dear old Charles Dickens has a lot to answer for!

Unsurprisingly, perhaps, there was an inference that Julia's parents were likely to leave the area, which now held so horrible an association for them. They had relatives near Walsingham with whom they could stay until they found something permanent. An older brother – William – seemed determined to remain: he worked on the farm which owned the wood where his sister had been attacked and clearly wanted to keep his job. Reading between the lines, though, I wondered if he saw himself as some kind of defender of his sister's honour and guardian of her grave.

I read on. An inquest had been opened and adjourned, and I wondered why one was deemed necessary when the cause of death was so obvious. Then I remembered the Select Committee and guessed they'd had a hand in the matter. Which reminded me to look again at the index.

It was neatly typed, almost certainly the product of a relatively modern electric machine. The paper, though foolscap rather than A4, was still clean and white and it struck me that the compiler might still be around. I summoned an assistant and asked him – in suitably hushed tones – if he knew who had been responsible for the indexing of the *Anglian Courant* volumes.

Rather to my surprise he did.

"That'd be old Miss Lessingham," he said. "One of our volunteers. Very thorough lady! She used to be the County Archivist at Norwich."

"Is there any chance of getting in touch with her?"

"Sadly not. I'm afraid she died a couple of years back. But she *was* 97."

Ah well … I nodded appreciatively.

When I asked if it would be possible to have photocopies of the *Courant* articles, he explained that they had a special large-format copier in the basement but it could only be operated by library staff. I was in no hurry so I marked the passages with slips of paper and decided to browse the shelves for further background while I waited.

I soon chanced upon a complete nineteenth century edition of the *Bacton Letters*. I had come across these in a Language Development module at Cardiff but had largely forgotten about them. It all came back to me now: the Bactons had been a major landed family in Norfolk during the later Middle Ages, with a spectacularly unusual degree of literacy for the period. They were serial letter-writers who had bombarded each other with correspondence for much of the fifteenth century. Miraculously, most of this had survived and was now regarded as a major primary source for socio-economic history as well as medieaval linguistics.

Pulling down the final volume I went straight to the index. Finding nothing under Old Snetty (of course he wasn't quite so old when the letters were written!) I tried *W* for Watkyn and was rewarded straight away. Volume VI: page 102; Sir Edward Bacton to his son Roger, an undergraduate at Oxford, dated Corpus Christi 1481. Exactly a century after the Peasants' Revolt.

… yt beyng noo full an hondred yeeres syns quhen yn tyme pastte dyvers goode ffolk of thys parties heredwellynge, peasentis bi degrie, rose uppe ynder yt worth-schyppfulle captayne yclept Watkyn de Snettyshame, there be noo mickle rumoure hereatte yt thyss sayme Watkyn be once moorre arisen ffromme hys grayve yn hys fflesche. An wyf of Dockynge declareth yt she held converse yn the maryshes wit an seeming fair hathel, most coutyouse yet wythalle in sackynge and ragges ycladden, and heftynge yt manner of glayve called Welsch Hook bi ye Ynglishe, like ynto an hedge-bylle. Methynkes thys be but devilische syperstiscyon …

Once I'd remembered that - thanks to the long retention of an Anglo Saxon rune - the letter Y was sometimes used to represent TH as in "this" or "that" - I managed to read it without too much difficulty!

He was clearly a level-headed fellow, this Sir Edward Bacton. I liked his style and carefully copied out the extract. As far as I could make out, it was the only mention of Old Snetty in the entire collection, although there were passing references to the depredations of Henry Despenser, Bishop of Norwich. One of the earliest letters, in fact mentioned a contentious litigation between Sir Edward's great grandfather and the said Bishop concerning a parcel of glebe land over towards Caistor.

Presently the assistant returned with the photocopies and I went in search of lunch. I was going to get my tour of King's Lynn after all.

It was a pretty shabby town really: at least that was my general impression. Once elegant Georgian terraces had seriously gone to seed, their paint flaking and stucco peeling. Cracked windows had been mended with plastic tape and a few broken ones were stuffed with old bedding. And this was within five minutes' walk of the historic centre and the huge old priory which might have passed for a cathedral anywhere else! Beetling, half-timbered merchants' houses jostled with sixties concrete and there was noisy, smelly traffic everywhere: no pedestrianisation that I could discover. Even the vast Tuesday Market – surrounded by some of the most graceful vernacular buildings I had ever seen – was demeaning itself as a mere car park when it should have been an open sea of cobbles.

And yet it had not lost its Hanseatic soul and there were places where real gems abounded. Closer to the river, ancient barns and warehouses lined the narrow alleys dipping down to the busy quays where, as I had observed from the boat, the ancient cause and purpose of this town was continuously manifest. Dutch gables and crow-stepped brickwork proliferated along the wharves and it didn't take too much imagination to substitute the steel coasters for Baltic cogges; Geordie brigs and Dutch botters and tjalks.

The baroque Customs House – quite breathtaking in its measured proportions and sugary detail – stood moated in its stagnant *fleet* where a couple of ancient wooden hulks rotted into the glistening mud.

I found a small pub full of nautical bits and bobs and enjoyed a passable chilli con carne before making my way back to the bus station.

*

That evening the three of us sat in *Samphire's* cabin, the boat rocking slightly as the tide began to lift her. A Tilley Lamp hissed on the table between us and I read extracts from my findings by its steady yellow light. O'Brien was listening very carefully, nodding now and again until I came to the report of the poor girl's death when his expression changed dramatically.

"What about the boy?" he asked sharply.

Peter and I exchanged glances: I hadn't yet mentioned a boy. Nor even a child, directly … though I suppose that was explicit in the reference to childbirth.

"The baby *was* a boy," I said carefully, trying not to sound as if I was trying to trip him up. "To be honest, I'm surprised they even revealed its gender."

"To protect his identity, you mean?" asked Pete.

"Exactly."

"No name given, I suppose." O'Brien said.

"Of course not," I replied.

"Fair enough," he nodded. "The poor kid's entitled to a clean slate."

"There was a brother too," I said. "Julia's brother I mean. William. It looks as if he stayed in Lingstead when the parents moved away."

"Ah yes," O'Brien mused. "*Bill*, she called him. I wonder where he is now?"

He sat still for a moment, drumming his fingers on the table, staring into space. Then, snapping out of his brown study, he announced that the following day we would look for Julia's grave.

*

It was well past midnight when we turned in but our skipper decided we should set watches this time … just so we got used to the idea. Again, there was no need for riding lights but he carried the Tilley Lamp into the cockpit with instructions to light it on the doghouse roof if we heard anything sounding like a boat approaching the creek.

This time I drew the graveyard shift as O'Brien called it: two until four. Actually I couldn't sleep much knowing I had to get up again so soon so, using a torch and trying not to keep Peter awake, I began to read O'Brien's book, of which we'd each been given a copy at last. It was quite well written and certainly caught the flavour of the fourteenth century without too many *Merrye Englande* clichés. It was a straightforward piece of historical fiction … a *ripping yarn* certainly, just stopping short of the proverbial *bodice ripper*. What it was not, however, was an examination of the supernatural legend. That, it seemed to me, was perhaps what we were doing now.

I dozed off about half way through chapter four and at two o'clock O'Brien shook me awake and thrust a steaming mug of black coffee into my hands.

"Your turn!" he said cheerfully, and I crawled out of the saloon.

A moon was up and the marsh, largely flooded now, glimmered with a million shades of blue and silver. The solitary barn was a humped silhouette and beyond it one or two village lights still burned, as if offering a feeble challenge to the stars. Turning to seaward, I could just make out the horizon of dunes … an ethereal grey in the moonlight. The sea itself was invisible, but I could certainly hear it; a constant susurration of sand; a backing track to the constant rattle of the reeds … sea and sedge maintaining an eerie discourse in the dark.

Black water rippled against the hull, chuckling slightly as the ebb sucked past. Birds squawked from time to time, both closely shrill and distantly faint. Some calls I recognised – curlew and oyster catcher – others I did not: corncrake or bittern perhaps? Owls were obvious, but still the most chilling of all. An occasional bat whiffled adroitly through our rigging.

The first hour passed without incident and a few minutes after three I felt *Samphire* begin to settle on the mud again. Then, suddenly, a pair of headlamp beams swept over the marsh and I heard the growl of a car engine somewhere to landward. The lights vanished and the engine cut out. A metallic door clicked open and shut … not loudly, but audible enough in the still night air. I could see no sign of a vehicle on the road past the barn but it could have parked further up towards the village.

At three twenty-six I saw it: a human figure creeping round the side of the barn. It paused, inky black against a blaze of stars. It was impossible to tell, of course, but I got the distinct impression that whoever it was, was watching us … though quite how visible we were now the tide had fallen I wasn't too sure. After a couple of minutes, and to my considerable relief, it retraced its steps and disappeared. About five minutes later I heard the car start and once more the headlamps swung over the marsh as it turned around and crunched away, its engine fading into the night.

I spent the remainder of my watch considering possible explanations: smuggling; poaching … witchcraft even. The only thing I could be certain about was that it wasn't Old Snetty … not unless he'd found time to take a driving test at some point since 1381!

I woke Peter at four and told him what I'd seen. He nodded solemnly but seemed more agitated about something else: "Last night," he whispered hoarsely. "He *knew* about the boy … before you'd even got to that bit!"

"I noticed," I whispered back. "Obviously he knows far more than he's letting on, but I think he knows he tripped up there. He's certainly playing games with us but we won't find out why unless we play along."

"I know," said Pete. "But I'm starting to feel even more like a puppet now."

"Me too," I agreed as I crawled back into my berth.

FIVE

Thursday's breakfast took a while to prepare because we had to use the small stove from the forepeak and set it up in the cockpit. The bank was far too soft now to support the larger model and none of us fancied spending too long on the rickety jetty. O'Brien had bought some bacon and eggs in the village the day before, and by the time we got it, breakfast was worth waiting for. Once again the sky was clear and we ate in the cockpit, watching a faint mist dissipating over the reeds, which we knew would be completely gone by the time sun cleared the church tower. I had been coming to the conclusion that a full breakfast in an old boat up a Norfolk creek on a sunny summer's morning was an experience second to none, but of course the shadow of death was upon us now, and the unspoken awareness that our skipper had not been totally straight with us had taken the shine off the idyll.

I told O'Brien what I'd seen on my watch and he just nodded gravely. Peter had nothing to add except that he'd seen an unusually bright shooting star, but he admitted to having dozed off at least twice.

It was clear by now that the tides were getting bigger even though the equinox was still a few weeks away. Peter explained that this could happen if high winds far out to sea were pushing large bodies of water inshore. The fact that we only had a mild south westerly here signified nothing: it was what was going on out on the Dogger Bank or in the German Bight that really mattered. It occurred to me that if we had a radio we could find out from the shipping forecast. I should have bought one in King's Lynn.

"It might be an idea to look for a higher jetty," he added. "We don't want to settle on the edge and topple over."

O'Brien said he thought there were a couple further up the creek, just beyond the barn. He was right, and after breakfast we used the dinghy to tow *Samphire* up into the head of the creek, between the barn and the overgrown stump of the windmill.

*

One of the more curious features of the north Norfolk coastline is that you only have to walk a mile or so inland and you can lose any sense of being near the sea at all. Once over the first gentle chalky rise, you find yourself in a totally pastoral world of softly wooded undulations, shallow green valleys, flinty little hamlets and acres of bright grain. How do you place it? It manifestly isn't north country, although parts of the Wash are almost on the same latitude as the Mersey. Nor can it be south country, when Norwich is further north than Birmingham. Even the term *Midlands* doesn't sound right, with its connotations of industrial sprawl. So East Anglia will simply have to remain East Anglia.

It is certainly *English*, but the old Teutonic England of the Angles and Saxons. How strange, then, that O'Brien should be so powerfully drawn to it. I looked at him now, striding ahead of us along the road, his shaggy red hair swinging and his spade-like beard jutting ahead. Then I remembered those Celtic Britons on the Snettisham sign and started to smile. Once upon a time everyone in Britain spoke Welsh; a fact I love to raise with any who will listen. Perhaps O'Brien understood this too. Irish is not so very different after all.

On reaching Lingstead we discovered that the churchyard had not been used for burials – other than of a few cremated remains – for over twenty years, but a notice in the church porch explained that the parochial mother church of St Edmund's, Peddersley, still had an active grave yard.

"Where's Peddersley?" I asked.

"Over the next ridge," O'Brien replied. Only a mile or two south of here."

Since none of the cremation plots carried the name Whitfield, we set out once more. O'Brien led the way through the village and forked left at a Y junction. Within minutes we were in open country again. Quite why we were looking for Julia's grave I wasn't entirely sure, but the landscape was enchanting and I tried hard to think of our little expedition as nothing more than a holiday hike.

But not for long.

O'Brien suddenly stopped and stared intently at a footpath running up the side of a small dark wood to our left.

"That's where it happened," he said quietly.

The three of us stood silently in the road, looking at the stubble beyond the open gate and the brambles under the eaves of the wood. Pigeons murmured in the branches. Then the roar of an approaching car made us jump for the safety of the verge. It came from behind, shot past and squealed to a gravelly halt a few yards ahead of us. It was a dusty red Cortina. The driver, a fair-haired man in his 30s, got out and paced vigorously towards us. To describe him as angry would be an under statement. He was positively seething.

"What do you lot want?" he bawled. "Can't you leave her be? Who told you where to come anyway?"

Before we could even begin to answer his questions he started to swear volubly and told us in no uncertain terms to get lost. Then he stopped, stared at us wide-eyed for a moment and shaking with apoplexy before turning on his heel and stamping back to his car. He drove off with a smoky fusillade of backfires … the bluish vapour lingering in the lane.

"No prizes for guessing who that is," murmured O'Brien.

"Brother William?" I ventured.

"Seems likely."

I think we were all quite shaken but we plodded on regardless, up the lane and over the slight ridge into the next hollow where the red roofs of Peddersley broke through the trees.

St Edmund's would have amply graced any illustrated calendar of rural England. Though not as big as the massive hammer-beamed, perpendicular edifices along the coast, it was an attractive pile of clunch and flint and boasted that most East Anglian of features: a round tower of at least Norman (or even Saxon) origin. There were more yew trees in the churchyard than I'd seen anywhere else and I wondered how many parish bowmen had been sent to Agincourt.

We poked about amongst the graves, quickly identifying the more recent examples. Most of these were of the now ubiquitous mirror-polished grey granite, which looks so out of place anywhere other than Cornwall or the Scottish Highlands. Julia's grave, however, was a plain rectangular slab of whitish limestone, unembellished with anything other than its brief inscription.

Julia Jane Whitfield

Maria Mater Dei

Ora Pro Nobis

Peccatibus

"What's the Latin … if it *is* Latin?" asked Pete.

"*Mary Mother of God Pray for us Sinners*," O'Brien replied instinctively.

Of course! He was catholic. Though whether devout, nominal, or lapsed … I had no idea.

"Well this tells us one thing," he said. "Someone still visits."

He stooped to pick up a white rose, withered and dry but certainly this year's crop.

"The brother, perhaps," I said.

"Indeed it is," said a voice behind us, and we all turned at once. An elderly clergyman, presumably the Vicar of Peddersley and its dependant parishes, stood there with a curiously solemn smile on his lips. None of us had heard him approach. He spoke again, possibly to spare us the embarrassment of having to explain ourselves. "I was just going to check something in the vestry when I saw you looking at poor Julia's grave. Do you know anything about her?"

"A bit," said O'Brien. "I was camping at Skolme when … *it* … happened."

"I see," said the priest," pausing for a moment. "Yes. Her brother comes here quite often. He didn't leave you know … when the parents moved away."

We nodded.

"Is he a fair headed chap who drives a red Cortina?" I asked.

"Yes. Why?"

"We've just walked over from Lingstead and …"

"Were you by the wood?" he cut in.

"Yes. He drove past and stopped."

The vicar sighed, then compressed his lips as if deciding how much more information to impart.

"Ah … hmmm … well. Did he say anything?"

O'Brien answered: "Quite a lot actually. Most of it unrepeatable."

"Well I'm afraid it would be," replied the Vicar. "Look, Bill Whitfield was really cut up about what happened to his sister – as anyone would be, of course – and he's still obsessed by the idea that her attacker might return to the scene of the crime … as they sometimes do, I'm told. He used to hide up there for hours on end … days, even … sleeping in that old hut … just waiting. He doesn't do it any more as far as I know, but if he sees anyone he doesn't know hanging around the village there's likely to be trouble.

"I'm not sure I should really be telling you all this. William is part of my flock. So it's hardly professional … but … well … I wouldn't want him disturbed more than he is already and, of course, I wouldn't want visitors to put themselves at any risk."

"We understand," I said, glancing at Michael. "We'll be on our way."

The Vicar looked relieved but had one more question: "If you don't mind me asking … just what *is* your interest in poor Julia?"

"Well it's Old Snetty we're *really* interested in," responded O'Brien, quite ingeniously I thought.

The Vicar's relief was now palpable.

"Ah … folklorists!" he smiled. "To tell the truth I don't think Old Snetty had anything to do with it, but you know what these country people are like, God bless 'em."

Peter had a final question too.

"The Latin," he said, nodding at the grave. "Isn't that rather Catholic?"

The Vicar was in his comfort zone at last.

"Ah, well now … St Edmund's used to be the highest church for miles around. In the *theological* sense, I mean. *Anglo-Catholic* if you're familiar with the term. In fact my predecessor was said by some to be *more papal than the Pope*! He certainly conducted Latin masses from time to time … without asking the Bishop's permission of course! I suppose if the congregation had all been of his persuasion there might not have been so much of a problem …"

"You mean there was a schism?" I asked.

The old priest laughed. Actually, I got the impression he was surprised I knew so church-specific a word as *schism*, but he had the grace not to say so.

"That's putting it a bit drastically," he replied, "but yes … there was a bit of a disagreement. The Whitfields were among his closest adherents, along with a couple of other families, but over half the congregation was less happy with his *smells and bells* and eventually the Diocese persuaded him he might be happier with a chaplaincy at the Walsingham Shrine. He jumped at the chance apparently, and the family – minus brother Bill – followed in his wake. And then I came along."

"And held things together, I hope!" said Peter.

"I hope so too," laughed the vicar. "Actually, I discovered that if we dropped the English Missal in favour the 1662 Prayer Book, everyone was happy. It was always intended as a compromise after all. Liturgically dignified enough to suit the traditionalists whilst stripped of anything smacking too much of Rome!"

We all laughed politely and took our leave.

On the way back to Turnham Staithe, O'Brien was even more pensive than usual. Perhaps he found the notion of Anglicans regarding themselves as anything other than Protestant confusing. But I felt there was more to it than that. We had intended to grab a pub lunch at the *Rogue Unhung* but he thought better of it and we managed to hot foot it back to the *Sloop* for a sandwich just before it closed for the afternoon.

We spent the rest of the day pottering about in the dinghy so that Peter could proceed with the chart work O'Brien had asked him to do. The skipper seemed anxious to complete this task as quickly as possible, with particular attention to the network of creeks between Salt Head Island and the mainland at Chesterfleet. When I asked him why he'd only bought the one Admiralty chart - showing the whole of the Wash - he explained that he hadn't managed to find anything on a big enough scale to mark the channels he was interested in and – in any case – even Admiralty charts needed regular updating.

I humoured him with a smile but I couldn't really see the need. Navigation by sight was easy enough around here so long as there was enough water in the channels. There were dinghies skittering around all over the place and dinghy-sailors rarely require charts. Unless of course – perish the thought! – he was contemplating some sort of night passage.

*

On Friday morning I finished my watch at eight, yawned, stretched and slumped back against the gunwale. I'd stayed awake easily enough simply because so much had been going on in my head: in fact it was only now that I actually felt tired. There were still so many unanswered questions, and even the answers O'Brien had provided were at best incomplete and misleading; or at worst just plain lies. I didn't really buy the idea that he needed my literary or journalistic skills in some way. He'd published his novel and it was a halfway decent effort: quite *good*, even. A need for Peter's surveying skills did make a kind of sense if he wanted to push *Samphire* through the creeks behind the island, but we could manage with a lead line and a sounding pole, both of which could be easily improvised from the assorted junk in her lockers. And why did he want to go through the creeks anyway? Our trip from Hunswick had amply demonstrated our ability to make a passage on open water.

All that aside, why was he looking so hard for Old Snetty? That would have made perfect sense before he'd written his book, but hardly afterwards ... unless he was planning a sequel, or a piece of non-fiction. A *True Crime* publication, perhaps. But in that case why not just come out with it and say so? I'd been pondering these things deeply since my watch began, but was none the wiser for so doing.

Over breakfast O'Brien was a different man. The cocky, self-assured Celt had given way to the morose Teuton. But we didn't need to push him for answers this time.

"Up till now," he began as he finished his second fried egg, "There has been no apparent danger – other than the obvious risks associated with sailing – and I have let you find things out for yourselves, one piece at a time. *Discovery Learning*, I believe it's called. Much approved of by educationalists. But things have changed. We've been spied on at night and verbally abused by an obviously unbalanced and potentially violent individual … however much we may appreciate the root cause of his distress. We are moving into uncharted territory – no pun intended – and it would be unfair of me to continue to withhold the full picture."

He paused and looked at us if trying to anticipate our reaction to what he was about to say."

"You see," he continued, with a wary edge to his voice, "I know who Old Snetty really was."

"Go on," said Peter softly.

"It was me."

SIX

I believe it was a full minute before anyone spoke.

Eventually, however, I managed to ask him to explain and he drew a very deep breath before doing his best to oblige us. At least I think it was his best. In any case it was all we were going to get for the time being.

"I've already explained," he began, "that my family spent most of their time on the beach during that holiday at Skolme, but I preferred to explore the locality on my own and that was how I first heard about Old Snetty. They told me in the pub that there was a book of local legend and lore for sale in the Post Office (it still had one back then!) so obviously I got myself a copy. It gave me quite a lot of background and even included that quote from the Bacton Letters you found in the Library. In fact I think it was that which really gave me the idea …"

"Of writing the novel?" asked Pete

"No. That came later. Remember the reference to a *Welsh Hook?* Well, a day or two after my first visit I walked back to Lingstead and blagged another pint at the pub. Then I set about exploring the surrounding lanes and fields and eventually came to the path by the wood I showed you yesterday. Naturally I was curious to see where it went so I followed it. After fifty yards or so it turned into the wood itself and ran up to an old shed in a small clearing. It was pretty much falling down and full of rusty old agricultural implements including … you've guessed it … a hedger's billhook. Just the blade, you understand. The haft had long gone. There was also a pitchfork with a loose head. I pulled the head off and replaced it with the bill and … lo and behold … one Welsh Hook! There was a pile of sacks and a few scraps of canvas too. This gave me an improvised tunic belted with old rope. Shoes were a problem – they always are for re-enactors – so I went barefoot …"

"On all those nettles and flints?" I said. "Ouch!"

"Being a romantic adolescent," he replied archly, "I was prepared to suffer for my art."

"What art?" asked Pete, with a look of genuine puzzlement.

"Ah well … that's just it! I'd transformed myself into Old Snetty in order to re-ignite the legend. My intention was to lurk around the village and its environs, popping up from time to time to give people a fleeting glimpse before melting back into the landscape. Scuttling past cottage windows or perhaps running across roads a safe distance ahead of cars. Or stepping out behind them to appear briefly in their rear view mirrors."

"And you actually did all this?" asked Pete, somewhat incredulously.

"Only the once," he said solemnly. "I'm sure you can work out when."

Peter and I looked at each other and the pennies dropped simultaneously.

"The day you rescued Julia Whitfield," I said.

"Exactly! I'd just finished disguising myself as Old Snetty when I heard somebody or something crashing through the undergrowth, then shouts and screams. Male shouting and female screaming. I couldn't make out much in the way of words apart from *No! No! No!* … coming from the girl of course.

"I rushed out of the hut and charged towards the sound of the struggle, wielding my billhook and yelling what I hoped would sound like a war cry. She was down and he was on her, trousers round his knees and hands round her neck – trying to stifle her screams I suppose. But he looked round when he heard me, tore away from her and scarpered, hauling up his trousers with one hand and keeping the other one balled in a fist in case I caught up. As I probably would have done, had it not suddenly struck me that looking after the girl was more important.

"She'd fainted when I got back to her but she gradually came round … terrified of me at first: I was still dressed as Old Snetty."

"She'd be terrified of *anyone* in those circumstances!" I said. "Especially a bloke!"

"Yes I suppose she would," he agreed. "Anyway, I did manage to convince her that I wasn't actually a ghost by changing back into my normal clothes in the hut. I briefly explained what I'd been doing but I don't think much of it really sank in. You know the rest from the papers."

Peter spoke: "Yes. You let her walk home on her own."

"That's not quite right," he said hastily. "I did offer to accompany her. Obviously she was very shaken and possibly injured, and we had no idea how far her attacker had fled. She let me walk her back to the lane, and a little way along it until her cottage was visible. Then she insisted I drop out of sight. She said she was afraid her family might think *I'd* assaulted her. So I let her go."

"But you were a prime witness!" I said. "The *only* witness, in fact! Did she never mention you to her parents or the authorities?"

"Of course she did. As Old Snetty. I think she understood what I was doing and didn't want to blow my cover."

"And you never went forward?"

"No. I respected her wishes."

"So you could carry on playing silly games in the woods!" snarled Pete, seriously contemptuous, now. Even I was surprised.

O'Brien stayed calm.

"Look … I understand how weird all this must look to you. And it was weird … I admit it! But at the time I felt I was doing the right thing. After all, I'd possibly just saved her life."

Pete sighed and shook his head, but clearly his anger was subsiding a little.

"And you didn't impersonate Old Snetty again?" I said.

"I didn't need to!" he laughed bleakly. "You've seen what the media made of it! Locals; nationals; tabloids! Radio and TV I believe, but we didn't have access to that on the campsite. Terrible signal – even for the car radio."

"You certainly re-ignited the legend," I murmured.

"Too right I did … though hardly in the way I'd intended."

*

We didn't do much that afternoon, the atmosphere between us having soured somewhat. I could tell O'Brien wanted to carry on surveying the creeks but felt nervous about asking Peter. Instead, he suggested we gathered samphire on the marsh to have with our evening meal. So we splashed about in the brackish water, plucking the rubbery green stems from exposed banks of mud.

Pete wondered off to the village in search of mushrooms and a bottle or two of cheap Spanish red. As soon as he was out of earshot O'Brien squelched over to me and asked – with genuine concern I think – if I thought Pete was likely to pack up and go.

I shook my head. "No. He's shocked that you failed to do your public duty as witness to a serious crime, but he recognises that you saved the girl. Besides, he's nothing to go home to, and you *owe* him, remember."

"And you?" he asked, staring me in the face: a rather unusual eventuality for him."

"Oh don't worry about me," I said. "You've given me the scoop of a lifetime and my editor certainly won't begrudge me the time off!"

He looked quite startled now so I did my best to assure him that I'd at least *try* to show him in a good light, and a rather hesitant flicker of cautious relief suffused his features.

That night, after a good supper of mushroom omelettes and fresh samphire (it really does taste like asparagus and certainly made a change from baked beans!) I took the second watch and something happened which reminded us in no uncertain terms that O'Brien wasn't the only one with unfinished business around here. From twelve until sixteen minutes past one I neither saw nor heard anything untoward. Although the weather had continued fair throughout the afternoon, there was now considerable cloud cover and neither moon nor stars shed any appreciable light. I could see no further than the width of the little creek into which we had drawn the boat; even the black bulk of the barn had vanished.

I knew it was sixteen minutes past one when I heard the shots because I happened to be looking at the luminous dial of my watch. They came in quick succession: two thunderous coughs followed by the raucous shriek of scattering wildfowl. Almost before silence had returned, I had considered the possibility of a fighter jet breaking the sound barrier and dismissed it. The RAF does fly training missions along this coast, but they normally go supersonic way out to sea and the resultant booms reach the shore as a low rumble. Those were shotgun blasts: I was certain of it. After all, I'd heard enough pheasant shoots in the woods around Hay.

O'Brien had woken but Peter had not. We shook him into consciousness and then all three of us crouched together in the saloon and conferred hastily in hushed tones. Poaching seemed unlikely given that it was probably too dark to see the game, let alone retrieve it from the marsh. You'd need a dog and I hadn't heard one, either barking or splashing about in the water. The shots could have been some kind of signal: drug smugglers communicating with each other? This seemed a bit drastic, though. Anyone might hear. Unless of course the smugglers were confident that the villagers would just assume they were poachers and turn a deaf ear to the shooting.

On balance – in view of our encounter at Lingstead Wood and the Vicar of Peddersley's warning - it seemed likely the shots were for our benefit.

"Could you tell where they came from?" asked O'Brien.

"Not really. I didn't see any muzzle flashes but – judging from the sound – I'd think down stream a bit. Nearer where we were …"

"That'll be it, then!" Pete put in. "That bloke you saw by the barn the other night was looking for us. The moon was up and we'd made no secret of our position."

"Casing the joint?"

"Yes. And he came back tonight without the car, went straight to where he'd seen us and emptied both barrels into what he thought was our berth. Or over the top, if he was just trying to warn us off."

"Then he must have walked past us," I said. "I swear I saw nothing … heard nothing. Didn't hear him leave either."

"Come on," said O'Brien. "He's a countryman! Probably *is* a poacher anyway. He'd know how to make himself invisible – and inaudible – on a night like this. Got to be that brother, hasn't it?"

"But his first visit was before he saw us at the wood," Pete put in.

"You can bet he'd heard about us, though," said O'Brien. "You know how news gets around in a place like this. Still … he can't have been too bothered about hitting us and – in any case – bird shot wouldn't have done that much damage to this old girl's timbers." He patted the deckhead affectionately.

"Probably not a good idea to sit with your head in a porthole, though," I remarked, and we all shuffled accordingly.

"If he's crazy enough to blast away in the dark," said Pete. "He's probably not too bothered about the risk getting caught. He might still be out there. Waiting."

"So what next?" I asked.

There was a moment's silence before Mike responded; a silence filled with the gurgle of the tide and the distant squawk of an owl.

"As long as we stay in this remote spot we could be in some danger. I suggest we get round to Chesterfleet or Boverey Staithe as soon as possible. As you say … he's bound to hear about it, but I don't think even he would be daft enough to open fire if we were anchored between a couple of expensive yachts with their owners on board. High water's in twenty minutes … just after two. So we'll slip our cables and drift out on the ebb."

"Round the coast?" I whispered. "At night?"

He shrugged: "There's a risk, certainly. But I have a plan and – of course – we've got Pete's superlative chart work, haven't we?"

Peter said nothing.

Then, rummaging in a locker, Michael produced the Ordnance Survey map, the Admiralty chart and Pete's roll of cartridge paper with its intricate contours, bearings and arcane figures and symbols. We partly unfolded the map and the chart so as to reveal only the relevant sections and still fit on the narrow table, whilst Peter unrolled his contribution on the berth beside him, anchoring it with a lifejacket at one end a cushion at the other.

O'Brien switched on a torch and shielded the beam with his hand:

the porthole curtains being very thin.

"I'd rather push through the creeks behind the island," he whispered, illuminating Salt Head with his torch. "But we haven't surveyed that far east yet and I don't think we'd make it in the dark. So we'll go round the outside. Open water, I know, but fewer hazards and we'll be way beyond the range of anybody's shotguns."

Well there is that … I mumbled to myself. "You said you had a plan?" I said out loud.

"Yes."

He swept the map and chart off the table.

"Peter; you version please."

Pete lifted his closely annotated roll onto the table and smoothed it out.

O'Brien shone his torch at his watch: "We've still got time for a little calculation."

"Calculation?" asked Pete.

"Yes. Thanks to this," (He tapped Pete's paperwork) "I can plot a course out of the Gut and into clear water, but I need to know precisely how long each leg will take."

"Depends what speed we're doing," grunted Pete.

"Say three or four knots. About walking speed, and we already know the scale you used here so it shouldn't be too difficult.."

"Erm … yes."

"So go on then."

"Me?"

"Well you're the mathematician!"

Pete shrugged: "Okay then. You lay off the course and I'll plot the bearings and times."

Another rummage in a locker produced parallel rules, a pair of dividers and a pencil. Using the parallels closed like a conventional ruler, O'Brien connected the minimum number of waypoints necessary for getting us out of Turnham Gut without going aground or hitting anything. Peter then scissored the parallels from each straight leg up to the compass rose he'd already drawn to collect its bearing. Then, using the dividers against the scale he'd drawn around the margins, he worked out exactly how long each leg should take in minutes and / or seconds. It looked like five legs linking six waypoints just to get us into clear water.

"Aren't you going to correct magnetic for true?" I asked, anxious to reveal that I did know at least something about navigation.

"Not necessary at this scale," he said. "If we were making a passage over to Holland, we'd probably miss and hit Denmark! The margin of error increases with distance run, you see."

"Are you sure you've never been sailing before?" I asked.

"Never. But physical laws are physical laws. If I can survey a field or a building site, I can survey a coastline."

I took his word for it, but couldn't help thinking there was one small problem: for all Peter's professional confidence, none of us had actually *done* anything like this before. And coastlines in this part of the world had a tendency to move.

I was dispatched into the stern to start the motor on command. We'd be less encumbered without the dinghy so O'Brien scrambled ashore, unhitched the small vessel and hauled it up onto the marsh itself, dragging her over the sodden samphire only to refloat her in a brackish pool where he made off the painter on a lumpy accretion of old concrete and rusty iron which had a vaguely wartime, defensive appearance. Obviously we were leaving quite a lot of gear in the dinghy, but he did manage to gather an armful of tins before returning.

Engaging the wheel with the motor cables so he could steer from amidships, O'Brien issued the order to start her up in a hoarse whisper. Pete knelt on a cushion on the floor where he could see both the compass and the clock. Both instruments were dimly lit with small green lamps designed to leave one's night vision unimpaired, but these were insufficiently bright for Pete to see his notes. Fortunately he'd memorised them. I pulled the cord and nothing happened. I pulled again and she fired second time, with a blatter which must have been audible for miles.

Equally fortunately, we'd already turned her round when we'd pulled her up to the head of the creek, so we simply cast off and pushed away from the landing stage and nosed back down towards the dark tunnels of leaning sedge: slow ahead.

Peter and O'Brien remained stock still, giving their instruments their full attention. After about forty-five seconds, Pete reached out and tapped the skipper's shoulder. The latter turned the wheel carefully, watching the compass all the time. The bows eased to port about forty degrees then settled as he met the drift with a deft counter turn. We began another straight run, this time for well over a minute before swinging to starboard again for a mere twenty five seconds, during which there was a soft grating under the keel as we slid over a mud bank.

I just made out a wall of sedge slipping past each gunwale: either they'd plotted our course with only inches to spare or we were quite literally up the wrong creek. Then I remembered how narrow the entrance had been in daylight. Bumping the bottom was not really a problem in itself as long as we bounced free again. It was getting sucked into the cloying mud as the tide fell which scared me. Then – when dawn broke - we'd be a sitting target. However, the next leg passed without incident; a good six minutes of gliding forward over still, black, water.

Then another turn: almost ninety degrees to port this time. And then a straight run of three and half minutes.

"Now!" hissed Pete, indicating the final turn to starboard which – if all was going to plan – would point our bows due north and the open sea.

Seven minutes passed and we began to feel the gentle beginning of a long corkscrew roll … a sure sign that the land was falling astern. The engine sounded different too: sharper … no longer echoing off the marsh. I upped the revs a little and we ploughed on, confident that the Pole Star was over the ship's head if only we could see it.

"We'll give it another five minutes," O'Brien said. "Then we should be well clear and we can head east. Keep an eye out for the beacon on Chesterfleet Point: rapid white flashes with a five second pause every fifteen. Oh … talking of lights, we'd best rig the runners."

"Runners?" asked Pete.

"Running lights. Red to port, green to starboard. Take the wheel a moment …"

He ducked away below and I could hear him sorting through the contents of the forepeak. Moments later he returned with a pair of copper lamps with coloured lenses, which he mounted on brackets either side of the coachroof.

"Only candle powered I'm afraid," he said, fishing a box of waterproof matches from a pocket. "But they are a legal requirement when under way in the dark. Let's have some sail up, shall we?"

Pete and I hauled up the canvass but the wind had fallen away considerably since our passage from King's Lynn. Still, the brown sail did make a slight difference so we left it bellying gently with the roll of the mast. I went forward and sat on the foredeck, my back to the tabernacle, resting my elbows on my knees in order to steady the binoculars I was attempting to focus where I judged the eastern horizon to be.

I'd read about the dangers of night-watch hallucination and it's true. After a while you start see what you expect to see … and sometimes things you don't. Only twenty minutes or so after screwing the rubber eyepieces into my own sockets I began to detect tiny flashing pinpricks of white light. But they were uneven and never in exactly the same position twice. Their inconsistency could be explained by the sea state: a swell rising to cut them off while I was still counting. Their changing position might have been a consequence of *Samphire's* corkscrew roll … but I didn't think that was sufficient to account for the lateral spread of the sightings. Perhaps it was lack of sleep or the sustained pressure on my eyeballs. Or I was seeing other - unrelated - lights as we rolled along.

Of course we weren't too far short of dawn, and I was anxious to pick up Chesterfleet beacon before it switched itself off with the sunrise.

Even as I fretted over the possibility of missing the light, I fancied I saw a faint wash of pink over the horizon ahead. I glanced at my watch. It was probably just the false dawn, but even that might be sufficient to obscure the stuttering wink of the beacon. I lowered the glasses and rubbed my eyes.

"There it is!" came Pete's voice from the cockpit. "To our right!"

"*Starboard!*" O'Brien corrected brusquely.

I looked to my right and sure enough a light was flashing rapidly a mile or so off our starboard beam. This time I did manage to count fifteen silver flashes alternating with a five second pause. Our speed over the ground must have been greater than we'd realised, probably because we had the set of the tide with us. Even as we stared at the beacon it was steadily slipping astern. To put it bluntly, we'd overshot the entrance to Chesterfleet harbour.

"Ready about!" O'Brien called, clearly intending to reverse our course and tack his way into Chesterfleet. I was about to respond with the classic dinghy sailor's retort of *lee ho!* when the engine coughed, spluttered, and died.

Had we been sailing properly … in a decent wind … this would hardly have mattered. But with barely enough breeze to fill the sail, there was no question of tacking into the strong ebb still draining out of the creeks and lagoons.

I clambered back into the cockpit as O'Brien lay on his belly on the afterdeck and examined the engine, burning his fingers on the hot metal.

"Seaweed in the intake," I suggested, this being a common problem with water- cooled outboards. It can usually be cured easily enough, by leaning over the transom with a scrubbing brush.

"Fraid not," grunted O'Brien, slumping back into the cockpit. "It's the petrol. We've run out."

"We've got spare …" I began.

"Oh yes," he said quietly. "We've got plenty of spare. In the dinghy."

None of us said anything, though I saw Pete stifle a gasp.

Recriminations were pointless. Sure … it was O'Brien's mistake but any one of us could have made it and, in any case, what mattered now was maintaining some sort of control over the vessel.

Peter helpfully pointed out that I was the dinghy sailor. Yeah … ten footers on a reservoir in the Black Mountains. "And you're the tidal expert," I responded. "Would I be right in thinking the long shore drift here runs east for a few hours? Especially on the ebb?"

"I think so. Yes."

"Good. With such wind as we have we can keep following the coast, and by the time we're approaching Boverey Staithe it should be light enough to see our way in. Michael; I assume there's a rudder somewhere? I appreciate you can't mount it at the same time as the motor …"

He stared into the bilges for a moment. "You're not going to believe this …"

Don't tell me! It's in the dinghy?"

He nodded feebly.

Even as I drew breath to scream, rant, swear or whatever, I spotted a paddle lashed under the port side bench and managed to stop myself. Small boats are no place for tantrums.

"Lash it to the shaft," I said, realising as I did so that I seemed to be taking control. *Three Men in a Boat* … and somehow I'd become Captain by default. O'Brien didn't seem to mind, but meekly retrieved the paddle and sorted out a length of suitable line.

"Talking of getting lighter," Peter remarked. "Shouldn't it be getting lighter *now*?"

"Yes it should," I agreed, looking around.

It was, in fact, light enough to distinguish between sea and sky, but only just, and we still couldn't see the flank of Salt Head Island that formed the coastline here.

Fog.

This time I really did swear.

I calmed down a bit when I realised that the sun was actually visible now. Well … a diffused pearly blob *I took to be the sun* was hanging in the pink wash to the east. The fact that we could see it at all rather suggested that the morning mist would burn off fairly soon. Perhaps it was a mere sea-fret rather than proper fog. At least I hoped it was. Still, as long as we pointed *Samphire's* bows at the pink glow we'd at least be heading in roughly the right direction for Boverey Staithe.

"Best run in closer to the beach," I said. "So we can be sure to see it."

O'Brien – who had now rigged the improvised rudder – calmly shifted the tiller a touch and our bows eased to starboard a little.

"You've got a lead line, I think," I stated confidently, having seen Peter and himself dabbling around in the creeks.

O'Brien nodded: "Starboard bench locker."

I rooted it out and handed it to Pete.

"Take a few soundings, would you?" I said. "We may get a rough position from the depth if we compare the chart with the tide table."

He nodded solemnly, while reminding me that the lead line was marked off in fathoms whereas the chart was calibrated in metres.

"Not too much of a problem, though," he said. "Six feet to a fathom; so that's – what? - roughly one fathom equals two metres?"

"I'll leave the maths to you," I said … meaning every word of it.

He took the line to the foredeck, and began sounding straight away, remembering to toss the lead well ahead of the bows and to start hauling the slack almost immediately so that the weight lifted free of the bottom as soon as the line was alongside and vertical. "Three fathoms!" he called back to us: "Six metres approx."

Plenty of water under our keel, then. I told Michael to hold our course for a few minutes more. He suggested raising the centreboard … somewhat tentatively for the boat's owner, I thought. I ducked into the saloon and reached under the table and shoved the leaver forward which retracted the blade. Picking up the Admiralty chart from my bunk I took it into the cockpit and taped it to the doghouse roof.

Peter swung the lead again, this time reporting half a fathom less: five and a half metres. At least this confirmed we were probably drawing closer to the shore, although it might have been an outlying shoal, of course. However, the chart didn't show any outlying shoals this close in.

"Keep going," I said to O'Brien, who was starting to look worried. But, as I pointed out, the only naturally occurring rocks for miles around were the brown boulders lying at the foot of Hunswick cliffs, which were well astern of us now. Even if we did run into the long beach on the north side of Salt Head Island, it would only be a gentle nudge into the sand.

"Unless the wind builds up," he muttered. "Don't underestimate the ship-killing potential of sand in a blow!"

"I think even I can predict there won't be a blow this morning!" I laughed.

"Two fathoms!" called Pete from the foredeck. "Twelve feet and falling."

"Okay, steer due east. Steady as she goes. Pete! Take a sounding every five minutes, please."

"Aye, aye, captain!"

That took me by surprise, but I was beginning to enjoy myself.

O'Brien changed course as bidden, but he had a look on his face which could have indicated either pain or relief. Or both.

The swell was still rolling in gently under our port quarter, glass-grey and totally without ripples, like undulating syrup. The sail flapped lazily but was still drawing enough air to pull us along half a knot ahead of the tide so we still had steerage way … just. Peter's soundings were consistent at two fathoms. According to the chart (adjusted to suit the state of the tide) that put us about a quarter of a mile off the still-invisible beach. So far so good!

Somewhat alarmingly, when the fog did eventually clear (surprisingly quickly as sometimes happens in August) the beach was still invisible. All three of us gazed to starboard.

No beach at all.

I was about to throw in the towel and admit that I'd totally miscalculated when O'Brien started to laugh.

"Perfect!" he cried. "It's the entrance to Boverey!"

With that he heaved the tiller hard over and we turned in our own length towards the bar between Salt Head and a prominent dune called Battery Sand according to the chart. The loose-footed sail dragged over my head as it slewed over onto its new tack. A boom, even in these light airs, would have had me over the side … possibly unconscious!

The bar was still covered but we felt it bump the keel and we dragged to a sluggish stop.

"Up centreboard!" called O'Brien, firmly in charge again. "And everyone overboard!"

We jumped into the thigh-deep water, got our shoulders under the gunwales and just about managed to rock her free before hauling ourselves back on board. It transpired that we'd made the tack just in time, because the wind died away completely now and we sat stock still in the shallows behind the bar.

"Can you see a windmill?" asked O'Brien, shading his eyes with a hand. I followed his gaze but there was still a residue of mist over the cornfields behind the village. However, when I raised my glasses, the dim silhouette of a brick tower – complete with sails – swam into focus on the ridge.

"I see it," I said.

"We've done it!" he cried. "Right on the button! Well done everybody!"

"We're not quite there yet," I pointed out.

He pointed to starboard where a lagoon-like sheet of water opened out behind the island.

"Cockle Hole," he said. "We'll anchor in the middle. I'm told it never dries out completely."

You can't row a cruising yacht; they are simply too wide. But you can paddle. O'Brien dismounted the makeshift rudder and handed me the paddle he'd used. He said there was another one somewhere, and it eventually turned up in his cabin. So Pete and I sat either side of the cockpit and paddled, Canadian style, until *Samphire* lay in the middle of the anchorage. O'Brien had already made his way onto the foredeck and stood ready to drop the hook. There was quite a splash as our galvanised CQR on a fathom of chain and plenty of hemp plummeted down through the pellucid water to the ribbed white sand beneath.

"Well done everybody!" O'Brien repeated.

Pete gave me a look and said under his breath: "Fine. So now we're organised, what do we do?"

I chuckled bleakly. I don't think O'Brien heard us, but a cheerful announcement that it was time for breakfast came down from the foredeck. Ten minutes later, a kettle was whistling on the small stove and he was emptying baked beans into a pan.

*

Once again we regretted the absence of the dinghy. Our anchorage was at least as far from the village as was our previous mooring, but here there was no road between the two. Depending on the state of the tide, the dinghy would at least have got us over to the footpath on the foodbank to the east of the channel … or even up to Boverey Staithe itself. So, if we fancied a run ashore, we'd have to swim. In reality, though, we were all dog tired, having been awake since I'd heard the shots in the wee small hours, and once breakfast was squared away we all retired to our bunks.

Even if our putative assailant knew exactly where we were, he wasn't going try anything in broad daylight. High water would be back around mid afternoon and O'Brien reckoned we'd be able to get *Samphire* up to some proper moorings in what was actually known as the *harbour* hereabouts. Safer still!

As I dozed off, Pete's rhetorical question about what we were actually going to do now we were here drifted into the forefront of my mind. I yawned and closed my eyes … far too tired to even think about an answer.

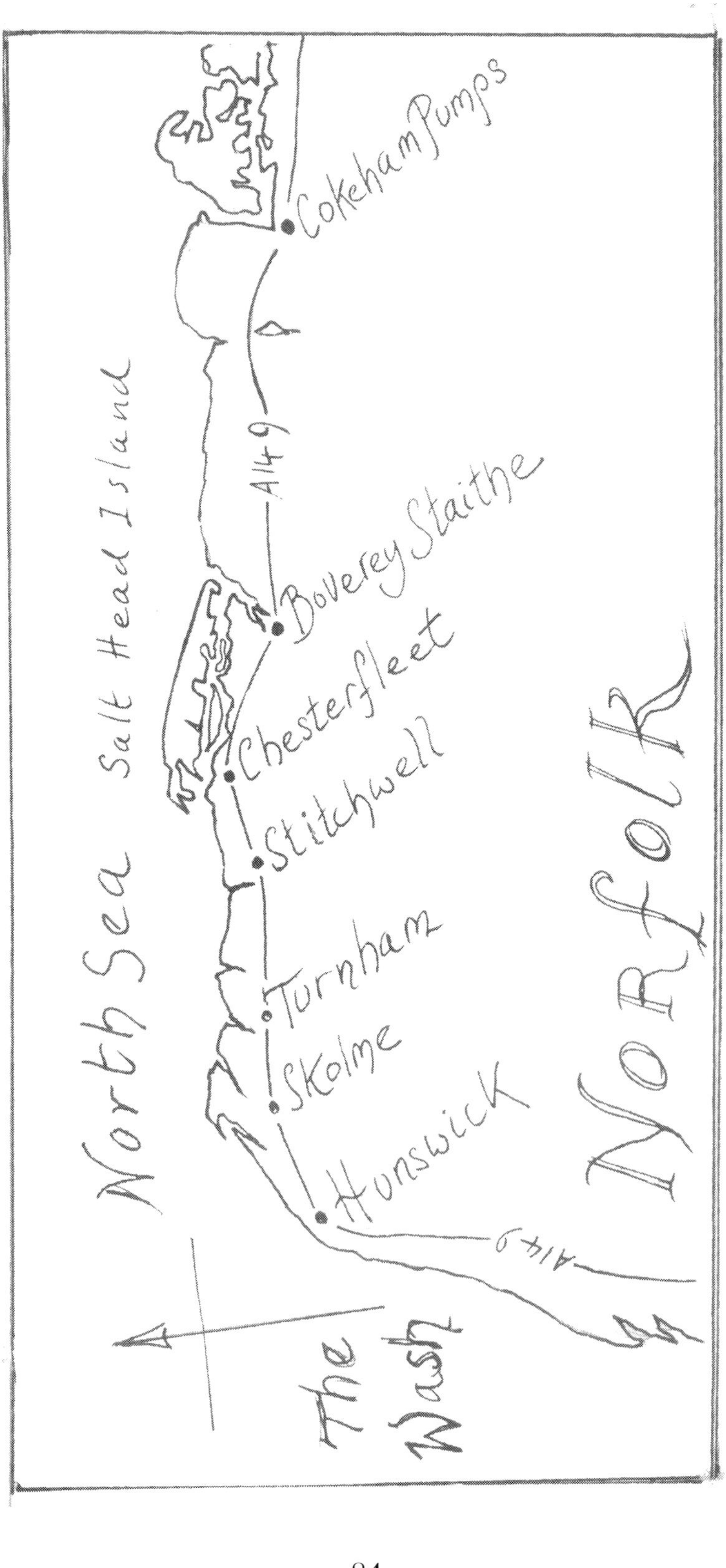
North Sea
Salt Head Island
Cokeham Pumps
A149
Boverey Staithe
Chesterfleet
Stitchwell
Turnham
Skolme
Hunswick
A149
NORFOLK
The Wash

SEVEN

Friday afternoon started with a bang.

Another shotgun blast.

Just the one this time and some distance away, so we weren't too worried.

"Must be a bit of wildfowling goes on around here," commented Pete.

O'Brien agreed but admitted that he had no idea when the open season was. I said I thought it was later in the autumn and – in any case – that sort of shooting tended to happen at dawn and dusk. He nodded and said he had a pretty good idea what was going on and there was nothing to worry about.

A few minutes later we saw what he meant. The tide had returned, the bar was invisible and the main channel was brim-full. There was a brisk breeze too: West South West; gusting three or four on the Beaufort Scale. A dinghy sailor's dream! There were small whitecaps on the lagoon and I noticed a circuit of little yellow buoys which I was certain hadn't been there when we'd dropped anchor … though I may have been too tired to notice.

"Watch the channel," said O'Brien.

From where we lay at anchor, a big bank of sedge obscured the view up to the village, but we could see where the creek debouched into the lagoon. Just as he'd implied would happen, a flotilla of small boats – mostly *Puffins* and *Optimists* – suddenly emerged from behind the reeds and began zipping around the yellow buoys like mounted Indians encircling a wagon in a western. *Samphire* was the wagon of course. Many were crewed by children whose consummate skill was quite breathtaking. They were followed by the larger classes; such as the *Mirror* and the *Enterprise*. Having once raced a *Mirror* on the Welsh reservoir in my teens, I succumbed to a fit of nostalgia and resolved to reacquaint myself with the sport at the earliest opportunity.

I glanced back towards the channel and saw a number of swaying mastheads and fluttering burgees over the sedge tops. The bigger stuff hove into view now; the *GP 14s* and the *Wayfarers*. There were faster boats too … slinky *Lasers* and *Fireballs* which wove in and out of everyone else with apparent ease … until a stately *Wayfarer* heeled just a touch too far and went over. One of the *Lasers* bounced over her mast and it wasn't entirely clear who'd come off worst: the *Wayfarer* with a severed mast or the *Laser* with a mangled centreboard! Something else wasn't clear either. Was this an open, multi-class race or a skilfully organised melee of simultaneous races? I reckoned it was probably the former as we'd only heard the one gun. Multiple races would surely have required multiple starts.

Once the cavalcade of boats coming out of the channel began to ease, O'Brien gave orders to weigh anchor and hoist sail.

I could still see some mastheads advancing towards the lagoon.

"Are you sure about this?" I asked.

" 'Course I'm sure," he responded cheerfully. "There's enough water for all of us now."

When we rounded the sedge bank into the approach to the village we saw there were still a few boats coming down towards us … older, wooden boats now, some not unlike *Samphire* herself. But we were the only vessel trying to make her way upstream; very much against the flow. With the wind in the west we were all on a beam reach one way or another, so we had to time our tacking to interlock harmlessly with theirs. This resulted in a sequence of *do-si-do* dance moves around every vessel we passed. Somehow we made it without hitting anyone but – had we done so – I don't think we'd have done too much harm to hulls as hard as our own. Naturally we apologised to each crew encountered, but they all seemed to take us in their stride. It was clearly a very relaxed affair, this local regatta, for all its inherent logistical difficulties.

Just below the village the channel turned sharply to starboard with a gravelly hard, covered with launching trolleys and trailers, to port. Opposite, the spongy saltmarsh – now barely showing above the tide – stretched back towards the island; a bleak contrast with the village foreshore where a colourful crowd of excited spectators and supporters milled around with ice creams and race programmes. Dogs and children dodged in and out of the shallows and land rovers growled up and down the rows of beached craft. The wind-chime effect of wire halyards ringing against alloy spars provided a musical soundtrack to the whole business of the regatta, and a few of the boats still moored in the fairway were dressed over all.

There was a stone landing stage in front of the long, low chandlery building, heavily buttressed with massive vertical timbers. We took *Samphire* alongside and tied up loosely for the time being. Some of the crowd drifted over to take a look, puzzled, perhaps, that we'd come in as all the other old classics were going out.

"Looking for a berth?" called an authoritative voice from above. We looked up and saw a stocky fellow in a fisherman's smock and waders. A peaked cap of stained denim was pushed back on his head and – somewhat alarmingly – a double-barrelled shotgun lay broken over the crook of his arm. But it wasn't Bill Whitfield. This chap was obviously responsible for starting the races.

"Harbourmaster," he called. "Steve Holkham. There's a few empty moorings further up. Take your pick. You can pay your dues in the pub later."

He pointed westwards where the creek appeared to peter out, but we knew from the chart that it kept dividing and subdividing into long, crooked fingers, each one curling and writhing deep into the marshes back towards Chesterfleet.

We thanked him, lowered the sail and cast off. It was much easier to paddle up to the buoys in the fairway than risk tacking across what was now an increasingly narrow channel. Finding a suitable buoy, we made up on it and relaxed. It was a mud berth, of course, and *Samphire* would take the ground at low water so we'd be able to get ashore with a bit of a squelch. O'Brien speculated that there were so many tenders lying around on the bank that we could probably *borrow* one without anyone being any the wiser. *Oh great*, I thought. *Let's add piracy to our litany of crimes*. I had a feeling you could still be hanged for it.

O'Brien boiled a kettle and brewed tea.

"So what happens next?" I asked between sips.

"You heard the man: we go to the pub to pay our harbour dues!"

"Any excuse!" said Pete.

"Of course! And if they do food we'll eat there. The kitty's still pretty healthy."

"But we've the rest of the afternoon to kill first," I pointed out.

O'Brien shrugged and spread his hands:

"We'll go ashore. It's a nice village and the chandlery's well worth a look. Oh … and there's somebody I need to see."

Pete and I glanced at each other with the raised eyebrows which had become an   almost instinctive reaction to so many of our skipper's more casual remarks. After all, it had never been a certainty that we were calling here. At least he hadn't actually said so.

"Someone you know?" I asked.

"Never met her before in my life!"

Before either of us could interrogate him further, we were hailed from the bank and turned to see the harbourmaster stepping down into the water and wading towards us. He was soon thigh deep, but his waders came up to his chest. Oddly, he had a boat with him and for a moment I wondered why he wasn't in it.

"Thought you might like to borrow a tender!' he called as he approached. "No extra charge … she's from the bone yard."

"Bone yard?" O'Brien replied.

"Yeah. Boats people leave behind, believe or not," laughed Holkham. "Wrecks, mostly, but she'll get you ashore and back a couple of times. Just pull her up on the grass when you've finished with her. She's going on the Parish Bonfire come November."

With that he turned and splashed back towards the bank.

The tender certainly was a bit of a wreck … or at least a derelict. All the paint had gone and the grey timbers were seriously warped and even split in places.

At least she's floating," I said.

"But we haven't seen it with anyone actually in it yet," observed Pete.

"Well, let's give it a try," said O'Brien, hopping over *Samphire's* gunwale into the tender. It was even smaller than our own dinghy and rocked alarmingly as he settled in the stern sheets. I seriously doubted that there was room for all three of us but somehow we squeezed aboard without capsizing. I happened to end up in the centre-thwart, which gave me the dubious honour of manning the oars. They were too short and very splintery. However, with Peter perched in the bows like a figurehead, we squeaked over the short distance to the flood bank.

O'Brien was right. Boverey Staithe was indeed an attractive and interesting place. Brick and flint abounded, along with orange pantiles and curvilinear Dutch gables. Cottage gardens positively erupted with flowers and there was even a house with a plaque claiming it had once belonged to the captain of a famous Tea Clipper.

O'Brien wondered off in search of his mysterious contact, so Pete and I decided to have a quick one in the oddly named *Aboukir Bay*. I hadn't really expected it to be open in the middle of the afternoon on a weekday, but it turned out that there was a special dispensation for the regatta. I asked someone about the race we'd got caught up in and it turned out I was right. It was an annual event called the *Wrecking Bowl*, open to any class of sailing boat able to enter the harbour. There was no handicap system, and no prizes for any boat that failed to sustain some physical injury. The eponymous *Bowl* was presented to the vessel with the most – or most severe – evidence of damage. My money was on the *Wayfarer* with the severed mast.

As we left the beer garden, Peter noticed that there was a portrait of Nelson on the inn sign and wondered how this related to the name. I vaguely assumed *Aboukir Bay* may have been one of Nelson's victories. He was a local lad after all.

Once in the Old Chandlery I decided it was about time I looked the part and bought a fisherman's smock and a peaked corduroy cap. Pete opted for a yellow nylon Kagoul.

"Expecting rain?" I asked.

"Well it's better than a mug with *A Present from Boverey Staithe* printed on it," he grunted.

Mercifully such things didn't exist. Busy as the place was, I got the impression that most folk present were fairly local or else members of a lucky cabal who'd stumbled upon the place as we had and been accepted and approved by the village elders.

O'Brien was waiting for us, sitting on the bank next to the tender. The tide was well and truly retreating now and it was obvious that if we all got in she'd stick to the bottom. Instead, we took off our shoes and socks, stashed them aboard. Then, rolling up our trousers, we waded back to *Samphire*, pushing the tender ahead of us.

"There *is* food at the pub tonight," I said once we were back aboard.

"Ah … you've sampled the delights of the *Aboukir Bay*, then?"

"Just a half each," said Peter.

"Very Sensible! Saving yourselves till later."

"You found who you were looking for?" I asked.

He nodded.

"Are you going to tell us who it is?"

"A lady called Bates. Anne Bates. She's the local secretary for a bird conservation group."

"I didn't know ornithology was among your many interests," I said.

"It's not really. But someone told me she once had something to do with the Whitfield family."

Here we go again, I thought. More random fragments of his back story suddenly sprung upon us out of nowhere. He must have been planning to come to Boverey all along. I sighed audibly.

"What's the matter?" he asked, as if my growing exasperation was somehow unreasonable.

"Who told you about her?" I snapped. "Where? When?"

Then Peter summed it all up with a statement – a long one for him - worthy of prosecuting councel, and it struck me that surveying probably has as much to do with law as it does with mathematics and geography.

"You lure us to Norfolk to help you uncover the truth about the ghostly reappearance of a fourteenth century outlaw. Then you admit that you knew the explanation all along. Moreover, in the course of that admission you let slip that you witnessed a serious crime but did nothing to help bring the perpetrator to justice … oh … yes … I do acknowledge that you probably saved a young girl's life in the process, but she died anyway – later - and you have done nothing to assist her grieving family since. In fact we have seen how your … *our* … presence on this coast has antagonised her brother and possibly placed us in harm's way. And now you slip off to make enquiries of someone as yet unknown to us, but whose very presence here suggests in no uncertain terms that you always intended to bring us to Boverey Staithe. Clearly there are issues you continue to explore, but – given your recent record in such matters - I think we can be forgiven for suspecting that, once again, you know very much more of the whole picture than you are allowing us to see. Quite frankly, Michael, this is simply *not on*."

Had it been possible to stand up straight in *Samphire's* low cabin, I was pretty certain he'd have gripped the tapes of his life jacket the way a barrister grips the edges of his gown.

O'Brien was breathing deeply now, clenching and unclenching his fists. He made several attempts to speak but broke off each time. It wasn't anger; I was pretty sure of that, but I wasn't entirely certain what it was. Frustration? Fear? At one point I thought he was going to burst into tears. … but he didn't. Above all he seemed in the grip of some kind of *indecision*. When he did eventually speak it was very quietly.

"Very well. Next time I go off to make enquiries – as you call it - you can come with me."

"When will that be?" I asked.

"Tomorrow."

"Where?" asked Pete.

"Cokeham Pumps … oh, don't worry … we'll take the bus. Now, for God's sake can we please go to the pub?"

*

The tide was out completely now so we walked ashore, sliding the tender like a toboggan, unsure if we'd need it on our return.

The *Aboukir Bay* was not quite as atmospheric as the *Sloop* at Turnham, but it was cheerful and friendly … full of sailors and their families swapping yarns about their performance in the *Wrecking Bowl*. Many were still in their yellow oilskins and salty puddles spread across the stone flagged floor. Apparently the prizes were to be awarded later. O'Brien went to the bar to get the first round in and discovered that the landlord was none other than Steve Holkham. (We discovered later that he was also a Voluntary Coastguard; the Chair of the Parish Council; Commodore–for-Life of the Sailing Club and a Church Warden for the *United Benefice of all the Boverys by the Sea*.)

I'd been hoping that O'Brien would open up with a few drinks inside him, the way he had in the *Sloop*, and reveal a bit more of the bigger picture. I think he might have done too, had we not been badgered by myriad old salts wanting to know why an obvious gaffer like *Samphire* was rigged as a lugger. O'Brien repeated the standard answers about safety and convenience when single handing etc.

"But there's three of you!" One of them protested.

"Not *usually*," replied our skipper.

At this point I thought we were going to be grilled about what we were doing here but our food arrived just in time. Lobster Thermidor and Duck a l'Orange to share. (We hadn't ordered it *per se*, but apparently it was what they always cooked on regatta night.) A ship's bell was rung vigorously: not for closing time but to announce the commencement of the prize giving and all attention was suddenly focussed on the dais which had been erected at the end of the lounge bar, upon which stood Steve Holkham … resplendent in a quasi-naval uniform, complete with cocked hat and sword. Raucous cheering filled the pub.

At least twenty crews came forward with a litany of damage and injury and all received copious pints of free beer, but I was right about the *Wayfarer*, whose skipper and crew were duly presented with the *Wrecking Bowl* itself. Said bowel (a rather nice piece of old red and blue Imari ware if I wasn't mistaken) was full to the brim with what looked like rum punch. The skipper and crew were obliged to drain it in quick time … which they did … to thunderous applause.

Then, just before the inevitable folk group ascended the dais to round off the night with an hour or so of sea shanties, the Commodore called for quiet and made a surprise announcement.

"Ladies and Gentlemen! Boys and girls!" (The place was crawling with children ... legally or otherwise.) "Tonight we have one final prize to offer, and for once it does not require evidence of injury or damage. Quite the reverse, in fact! Ladies and Gentlemen, please put your hands together for the master and crew of the yacht *Samphire* who – against all the odds – somehow managed to navigate their fine vessel up the creek this afternoon without so much as a scratch to her – or to anyone elses' – varnish. For this redoubtable feat I am pleased to award them free mooring for three nights ... and ... " (He looked around for something suitable, settling on a random piece of Clarice Cliff from a nearby shelf) ... "I hereby initiate ... from this day forth and for ever ... the *Visitors' Vase!*"

Suddenly we were subject to another storm of applause as the band started belting out Ewan McColl's *Shoals of Herring*. They paced it unusually fast, but it was soon evident that dozens of people were planning to dance to it.

It was only a matter of time before we were too.

*

It was beginning to spit with rain as we made our way back to the boat.

There was sufficient water in the creek to require the tender, and as we bumped against *Samphire's* hull there was a distant peal of thunder far out to sea. Despite the continuing breeze, the air temperature was still high. A summer storm seemed likely and O'Brien sniffed the muggy air, confidently predicting that the following day would be cooler.

EIGHT

He was only partially right.

Although I was woken around five by the steady roar of rain on the coachroof, when I stuck my head out into the cockpit the air was just as hot and humid as it had been when we'd turned in. O'Brien was clumping around in his waterproofs, tying things down and checking tackle. We'd agreed that a watch wasn't necessary on this mooring, but I suppose he was woken up by the downpour just as I had been. Eventually he crawled back into his coffin of a cabin and I, too, drifted back into uneasy sleep.

Two hours later we were all up and having breakfast in the cockpit. The rain had stopped and the sun was reappearing through departing clouds. *Saturday!* I thought to myself: a whole week since I'd set out from the Welsh Marches. It seemed like a lifetime ago.

Yesterday, O'Brien had said we could both accompany him to Cokeham Pumps for the next stage of his investigation. In the event, though, Peter kindly offered to return to Turnham Staithe by bus and collect a couple of cans of petrol from the dinghy. I wasn't entirely sure about the legality of bringing fuel back on public transport and suggested he scrounge a lift or use a taxi for the return journey. O'Brien enthusiastically took him up on his offer because – although we could probably get petrol more locally – the fact remained that we had nothing to put it in.

I also suspected he didn't want to overwhelm his next contact by turning up mob handed.

Cokeham Pumps just about qualifies as a real port. It must surely be the only harbour between King's Lynn and Great Yarmouth which can still accommodate modern commercial shipping … and even then only at certain states of the tide. When we alighted from the bus there was a small Danish coaster sitting on the mud under a grain hopper over the only quay. Even so, it still felt more like a village than a town, with its grid of terraced cottages and shops, many of them colour-washed in a vaguely Cornish fashion.

We turned into a surprisingly steep street - well, steep for Norfolk - running away from the quay into centre of town. It was lined with fishing tackle suppliers; second-hand bookshops; hardware stores and antique dealers. Most of them, in fact, also sold postcards and beachwear … whatever it actually said over the doors. So actual tourism was clearly part of the local economy here, which was hardly surprising really. It was indeed a charming little place.

O'Brien kept glancing at the back of an envelope as we zig-zagged through the network of similar lanes and alleys, finally emerging at the end of a large rectangular green lined with venerable old trees on three of its four sides. Behind the trees stood what had to be the most genteel properties in Cokeham. It was not that Cokeham required an *oasis* as such, but this delightful, shady green space simply exuded calm.

"Here we are," O'Brien announced. "Number 17. Should be about … *there*."

He pointed diagonally across the luxuriant grass and strode off towards the far corner.

Number 17 was an architectural gem. Though relatively modest compared with some of its neighbours, it was elegant to the point of Georgian perfection. The walls had been rendered and painted a very pale sage green whilst the quoins, windowsills and lintels gleamed as white as fresh icing sugar. A pair of white columns supported a delicately pedimented porch which, in turn, supported a single Grecian urn. The door beneath was panelled oak but polished to a mirror shine. I wondered how on earth this was achieved in view of the relentless salt-laden wind. O'Brien gripped the (doubtless original) bell-pull and we heard a tinkling chime somewhere within. I stepped back a little so as not to crowd the steps.

The door was opened – not by a cadaverous butler as I'd half expected – but by an elderly but healthy-looking gent with pink cheeks and snowy whiskers. He was wearing tweeds and a maroon tie patterned with assorted wading birds.

"Mr John Hardacre?" O'Brien began.

"Yes?" came the reply, with an enquiring smile.

"Erm … Miss Bates … at Turnham sent us …"

"Of course! Messers Wilberforce and Thompson. The new members! Do come in."

Hardacre stepped back into the spacious hall and gestured us to follow.

"In there," he said, pointing to an open door. "Do please sit down. I'll be with you in a minute. Tea?"

We both nodded and entered a nicely proportioned but desperately untidy drawing room. "*New members?*" I whispered as we sat on the only two chairs which were not buried under piles of books and magazines. O'Brien just shrugged. I looked around: the walls were heavy with framed ornithological prints, including a few Thomas Bewick woodcuts that looked suspiciously original. There were stuffed birds too, but high up in glass cases on top of rosewood bookcases full of rich leather spines.

Hardacre reappeared with a silver tea service and made room for it on the corner of a huge mahogany desk, which was otherwise strewn with papers. Then scooping up a pile of magazines from the button-backed captain's chair behind the desk, he sat down and began to pour the tea.

"Anne *did* mention something about you," he began. "New to the area I believe? Anyway … splendid to have you aboard …"

O'Brien interrupted politely: "Mr Hardacre, I'm sorry but I think there's some confusion here! My name is Michael O'Brien and this is my friend Evan Price. Did Miss Bates not let you know we were coming?"

Hardacre frowned, pursed his lips and pulled at an earlobe. Then he looked up with a vaguely embarrassed grin on his face.

"Well she *may* have done," he said. "In fact she probably *did*. It's age, you see. Short-term memory and all that. You'll have to remind me what this is all about!"

O'Brien smiled and nodded patiently. "We're just trying to find out something Miss Bates thought you might be able to help us with."

Hardacre looked genuinely surprised, but not unfriendly.

"Well, if I can … of course I certainly will."

"Thank you sir." O'Brien began. "You will remember the Lingstead rape, I expect?"

"I'm sorry? Oh … Lingstead … of course. Years ago, wasn't it?"

"About ten. Well, you see, I knew Julia Whitfield … the poor girl who died. It was a terrible business of course, and there are … certain aspects … which I've never fully …"

"Mr O'Brien!" interrupted Hardacre, starting to look at us suspiciously for the first time. "Before you go on it's only fair to inform you that I was solicitor to Julia's family at the time. Retired now, of course, but you will appreciate there are matters which must remain confidential …"

"Absolutely!" cut in O'Brien, with what he obviously hoped was a reassuring smile. "I *know* you were, and that's precisely why Miss Bates recommended you to me. She knew you had the family's best interests at heart … as do I."

Hardacre sipped his tea and regarded us carefully over the rim of his cup.

"You know what Anne's connection with Julia was, I take it?" he asked at length.

I was secretly praying that the question wasn't addressed to both of us because I hadn't the faintest idea what the answer might be. In fact, I was beginning to wish I'd stayed in Boverey or gone back to Turnham with Pete. Once again I was feeling like an actor live on stage without a script … either in my hand or in my head.

But naturally O'Brien had an answer ready: "Of course. She was teaching at Lingstead Primary when Julia was there. She knew the family and stayed in touch when Julia went up to secondary school in Hunswick."

Quite how he knew about Ann Bates in the first place was anybody's guess. Frankly, I was beginning not to care.

But Mr Hardacre's expression brightened. "She's a good woman, Anne Bates. Dozens - no, hundreds – of people remember her with gratitude and affection. She spent her entire career in that one school.

Probably taught three or four generations of the same families. That's a kind of dedication you don't see much these days."

"You could always ring her if you want to check us out," O'Brien suggested.

"I could … but … well … if Anne Bates sent you I suppose I'd best try to help you … in so far as I am legally and morally able."

But he didn't sound entirely convinced.

O'Brien smiled a cleared his throat.

"Thank you, sir. Let me stress you're not obliged to tell us anything. We're not here in any official capacity at all; in fact Mr Price here has nothing to do with it really. He just a friend who's been helping me out with a few technical matters."

I nodded with what I hoped looked like supportive agreement but was in reality closer to relief that he was apparently distancing me from the case a little … despite my journalistic interest.

"Very well," said Hardacre. "Fire away."

"Julia had a child …" O'Brien began. "As a result of the rape, I mean. A boy, I believe. I never really got to hear if he survived."

Any relief I'd felt a minute or two back was snuffed out and dissolved like thin smoke: O'Brien was telling a downright lie. He knew perfectly well the boy had survived. I almost drew breath in order to blurt out a protest but managed to hold my peace. Whether out of cowardice or loyalty I wasn't sure. I was sure, though, that I was going to give him a hell of a grilling as soon as we were outside again.

"I see," said Hardacre, looking solemn now but offering a slight shrug with his answer. I thought I detected a kind of realisation – or resignation perhaps – in this faintest of gestures. I also may have begun to realise something myself … but I'm not sure.

Hardacre continued: "It is, of course a confidential matter at a *personal* level too – for me - but I am not aware of any attempt to conceal the fact that the child survived, as you put it. I believe it's all in the public domain."

"But does he know he's adopted?" O'Brien asked.

"Why do you assume he was?" Hardacre responded.

O'Brien looked suddenly flustered; as if caught out, somehow.

"Erm … it would be usual in such circumstances … would it not?"

Hardacre sucked his lips for a moment.

"Possibly. But Norfolk families are very close, you know. It might be more usual – especially a decade ago – for an unintended child to be brought up by its mother's mother … or any grandparent, for that matter."

"So he could have gone to Walsingham with the rest of the family? Except the brother, of course."

"Oh … you know about William, then?"

O'Brien chuckled: "Oh yes. We certainly know about William Whitfield, but don't worry … we're doing our best to give him a wide berth."

"Probably wise," muttered the retired solicitor. "As a matter of fact the lad didn't go to Walsingham with his grandparents. You were right, Mr O'Brien … he was adopted and - to be quite honest with you – I don't actually know if he knows! I helped them handle the legal side of it, of course, but once it was done and dusted it was totally out of my hands. His adoptive parents may have told him; or they may not. Either way, I have no say in the matter or knowledge of the choice they made."

O'Brien ruminated for a moment: I could tell he was building up to something important but probably difficult for Hardacre to square with his conscience. I could almost hear the cogs clicking round as he worked out how to phrase it gently but effectively. In the end he chose to phrase it as a question and I was just as taken aback as was the solicitor.

"If I wanted to see the child, would there be any legal means by which I could do so?"

Hardacre stared at him: a slight gasp parting his lips. I almost gasped myself. Then, quickly regaining his composure the solicitor said, "Well, you would have to convince Graham's adoptive parents …"

He stopped; open-mouthed and aghast as he realised what he'd said.

"*Graham*," repeated O'Brien quietly. "Don't worry sir … that's only a Christian name, which isn't much use on its own, and I know you can't possibly *tell* me the rest."

"Certainly not!" snapped Hardacre, struggling to regain his composure. "At least not without asking his adoptive parents' permission. Naturally they'd want to know who you were and why you were asking. They've heard of you, perhaps?"

O'Brien shook his head apologetically. "Not directly, but if they've heard of *Old Snetty* – which I know they have – then that would have to do."

"Old Snetty?" asked Hardacre, knitting his brows in puzzlement for a moment … before bursting into laughter. "Come now, Mr O'Brien! You surely can't expect me to trouble them with that old nonsense!"

"No," said O'Brien softly. "I don't suppose I can." He started to rise: "Well, thank you very much sir; you've actually been most helpful."

"Dashed if I know how," the old man muttered as he hauled himself to his feet and began to show us out. I knew we'd seriously disturbed his morning and discomforted his equilibrium somewhat, but he still had the courtesy to shake our hands. It was in his nature of course: he was one of the *Old School*.

Then again, he'd probably faced tougher competition than Michael O'Brien across a courtroom from time to time.

*

Neither of us spoke until the door had closed behind us and we were well out of earshot of the house, but by the time we reached the middle of the green I could restrain myself no longer.

"You *lied* to him!" I bawled. "Why?"

He stopped and turned, with a look of bewildered astonishment across his face.

"*Lied?* When? How?"

"About the boy!" I shouted, giving vent to my exasperation at last. "You *knew* he'd survived … so why ask?"

He frowned, and for all my pent up rage I could still see that he was genuinely trying to get his head around my accusation. Suddenly he threw back his head and laughed, clapping his hands on my shoulders.

"I *see!*" he exclaimed, recovering his breath. "Well yes … I knew he'd survived his *birth* … of course I did. That was in the papers as you know. But I didn't know for how much longer, or that he'd been adopted …"

"But we *talked* about the adoption!" I cried, heroically resisting the urge to knock his hands away.

"No," he said. "We *speculated* about it. In fact, if I remember correctly, *you* speculated about it more than I did. Anyway … it appears we were quite right. John Hardacre's just confirmed it hasn't he? And – going by what Anne Bates told me yesterday …"

"And there's another thing!" I blurted. "How did you know about her? And how to find her?"

"Julia told me. She was her pupil, remember?"

Now I was beginning to lose the will to live.

"But you only knew her for five minutes!" I protested.

He put his hands back in his pockets and shrugged: "You can learn a lot in five minutes. But actually it was a bit longer than that."

"Anyway, you were about to tell me what Ann Bates said? Did she tell you the boy's name?"

"No. That was the one thing she insisted I spoke to Hardacre about. I was going to ask him but he let it slip before I needed to. Poor chap must be mortified, but at least it saved me the embarrassment of pushing his professional integrity too far. He did it for me!"

"It was only a first name," I reminded him. "There must be hundreds of Grahams in Norfolk."

"True. But not all ten years old and living on the coast."

"How do you know he lives on the coast?" I asked.

"Look … I'm starving," he replied. "Ten years ago there was a brilliant chippy on the quay. Let's go and see if it's still there, shall we?"

"Okay," I sighed. I knew well enough now that pushing him was useless. He'd come clean eventually.

Twenty minutes later we were sitting on the quay wall with our fish and chips open on our knees. I had to agree the quality was excellent. A very large herring gull with bright beady eyes thought so too and was edging closer by the minute.

"Unchanged in a decade," O'Brien said with his mouth full. "You were asking about what Ann Bates said?"

"Oh … yes. I was." He'd caught me by surprise again.

"She told me very little outright," he continued. "But she implied a great deal. Remember she's a keen ornithologist. Naturally she knows all the other ornithologists along this part of the coast … people like John Hardacre, of course. Anyway, four or five years after the tragedy, the chap who ran the bird reserve on Salt Head Island moved on so the post became vacant. Hundreds of applications of course; a cottage comes with it, you see. Very remote, but ideal for any suitably qualified person who loves birds and solitude.

"As always, most of the applications were from dreamy romantics who didn't actually know very much about birds, but they settled on a young couple called Sykes who'd already managed a similar project on Gibraltar Point over by Skegness. The only potential difficulty was their young child …"

"Who was adopted?" I cut in.

"Exactly. But that wasn't a problem in itself, of course. No, the trustees of the charity running the reserve felt the cottage wasn't suitable for a toddler. How would it get to school when it was older, and so on? Actually, I suspect they may have been afraid they'd be held liable for its welfare in some way. However, the Sykes offered to modify the cottage at their own expense and … better still … they owned an old American Duck!"

"A what?"

"That's D.U.W.K … an amphibious military vehicle. A sort of floating jeep from World War Two. So – in all but the roughest of weather – they could drive him all the way to school and back regardless of the state of the tide. Ann Bates offered to put him up on the mainland when necessary and the Trustees were won over and Sykes got the job."

"And you think the lad is Graham Whitfield?"

"Well … Graham *Sykes*, yes."

"But she didn't actually *tell* you in so many words?"

"No. As I said … she deferred to John Hardacre for that. But think about it, Evan! Why tell me about the Sykes at all if she didn't want me to find out? What would be the point?"

"But what I *still* don't understand," I persisted, "is why she told you anything at all."

"Well, for Julia's sake, of course."

"That's precisely what I don't understand," I muttered quietly … just before the herring gull struck and clattered away over the harbour with half my battered fillet of cod hanging from its bright yellow beak.

O'Brien hooted with laughter and I found myself joining in, but I knew that my hooting had a somewhat manic edge to it this time.

"Come on," he said, rolling up his chip paper and looking around for a bin. "We'd best get back to Boverey. If Pete arrives before us he'll use the tender and we'll have to wade! Hope he found the petrol alright. We may need it tomorrow."

"Are we going somewhere?"

"Salt Head Island, I think."

"You're looking for the boy aren't you?"

"Well I certainly haven't come all this way to give up now."

"But why?" I asked. "You're surely not going to track him down and confront him with the sordid details of how he came to be in this world?"

"Of course not. But there's something I need to do there. And it wasn't *that* sordid …"

"What do you mean *not sordid!?* A teenager brutally raped and …" I broke off, largely because I was overwhelmed by the import of what he'd just said and partly because I suddenly realised I was shouting again. This time trippers with ice creams were stopping and staring.

He glanced at his watch. "Bus in five minutes, Evan."

With that he turned away and started walking. I stared at his back for a moment, hesitating. Realisation – when it dawned – wasn't so much a light bulb over my head as a whole bank of stadium floods crashing into blazing life. I could swear the ground shook too.

How could I have been so dense?

The child was his.

Obviously.

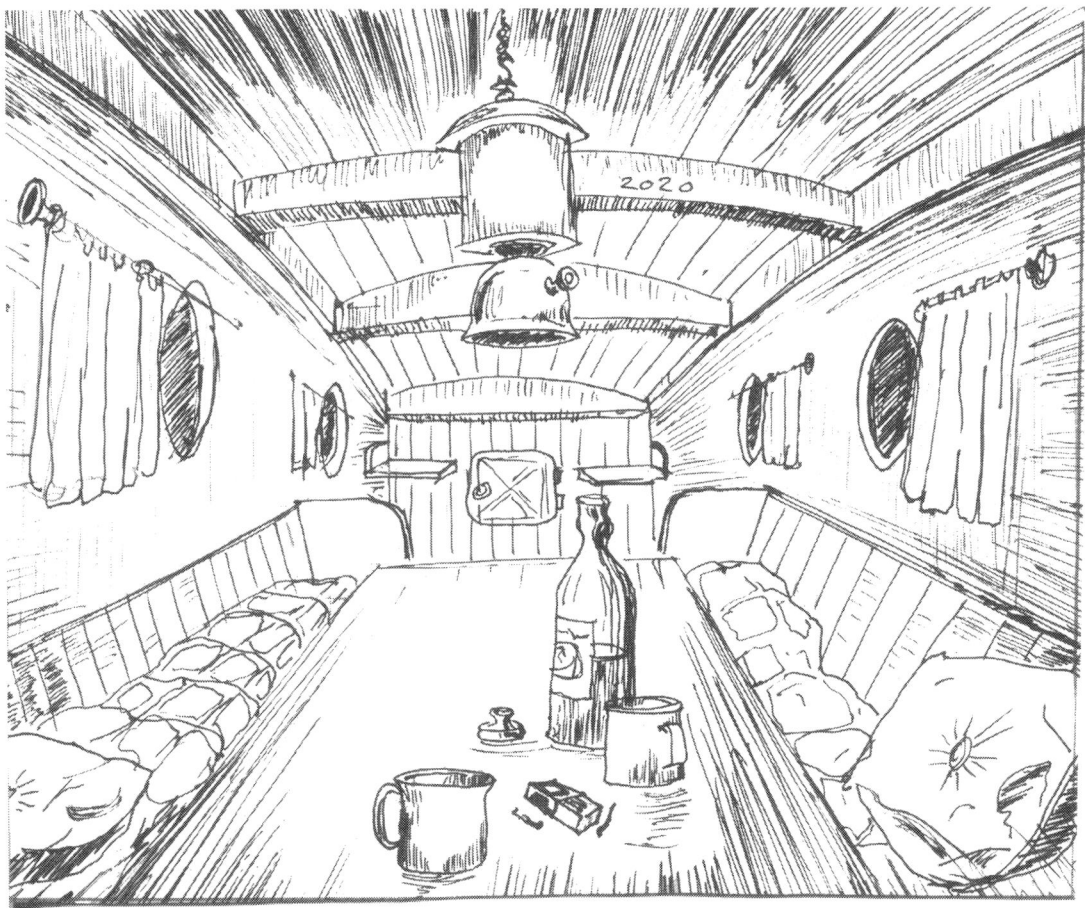

NINE

We barely spoke to each other on the bus back to Boverey Staithe. The sky was clouding over now and drizzle was beginning to streak the windows. We crawled westwards with the brown marshes to our right and the long wall bounding the Cokeham Hall estate to our left. The deer park was heavily wooded and overhanging trees brushed the upstairs windows noisily. Traffic was heavier than usual … locals heading for a Saturday night out in Hunswick or Lynn, I supposed.

By the time we reached Boverey the drizzle had evolved into the proverbial stair rods, lashing earthwards and rebounding on impact, and as we got off by the *Aboukir Bay* it was supplemented with a dose of bullet-like hail. We crossed the road and ran down the lane towards the hard where a blue light was pulsating amongst the trailered dinghies. For a moment I thought it was some sort of navigation light I hadn't seen before … until I realized it was mounted on the roof of a police car.

There was a shout from our left. The harbourmaster was standing in front of the Old Chandlery, in an oilskin cape and sou'wester this time. He was gesturing wildly for us to join him. We splashed over and followed him into the big shop with its tarry smells and nautical clutter. Two uniformed policemen were waiting inside.

"Mr O'Brien?" asked one of them, apparently making eye-contact with me specifically.

I pointed to Michael.

"Ah … I'm sorry sir." Then – clearly addressing both of us – he suggested it might be best if we all sat down. Steve Holkham had already arranged three folding chairs around a trestle table.

"Sergeant Garry Edwards," said the policeman. "And this is my colleague, PC John Rix. Traffic Division."

Holkham said he'd make tea and withdrew to a kitchen somewhere at the back of the shop.

Obviously the police were on the point of breaking bad news but I was confused. "Traffic?" I said vaguely. "But we've no cars here …"

"Oh … nothing to do with that sir," Edwards said hurriedly. "Er … we believe you've had a friend with you aboard your boat? A Mr Peter Rufford?"

Michael gave a slight start. "Peter Rufford, yes," he agreed quietly. I nodded in support.

"I'm really very, very sorry to have to tell you this," Edwards began. "But there's been a major accident …"

"But he's *still alive*," cut in the PC, anxious to provide the one crumb of comfort his sergeant had so far omitted.

"Yes!" the sergeant agreed hastily, covering his back. "*Alive*, yes. But in hospital of course. King's Lynn. In a coma. Multiple injuries. They used a chopper from RAF Marham …"

O'Brien seemed utterly rigid, staring blankly at some indeterminate point between and beyond the two policemen. His eyes were glazed; his mouth half open and the colour had drained from his face. I couldn't even hear him breath but his hands started to open and close: tight fists to open palms and back again with fierce regularity.

"What happened?" I asked, trying hard not to lose it myself.

"Mr Rufford was in a taxi heading this way," said PC Rix. "There's a blind bend just this side of Chesterfleet. There'll be a full investigation of course, but as far as we can tell at the moment the driver did nothing wrong …"

"So I should hope … in a taxi!" I exclaimed unnecessarily.

"Quite. But somebody else did. A Ford Escort coming the other way overtook on the bend. Head on, I'm afraid."

"What about the driver?" I asked. "And the other one, of course."

Rix glanced at the sergeant, obviously hoping his superior would shoulder some of the responsibility this time.

Edwards nodded grimly. "Both dead, I'm afraid. Instantly, we think. Your friend was very, very lucky."

"But will he survive?" I asked … knowing that he couldn't possibly tell me.

"Well that's a bit beyond our expertise," Edwards replied. "But I can assure you that KLG will do all it can."

"Was there a fire?" I asked. "Explosion?"

Edwards frowned: "Explosion? The tank, you mean?"

"That kind of thing, yes."

"No sir. That's much rarer than most people imagine. Thank God!"

"Right," I murmured, thinking about the two jerry cans of petrol which would have been in the boot. It was lucky no one had run into the taxi from behind.

"Look," said Edwards, "we can take you to Lynn if you like; we're going back shortly."

I looked at Michael, who now appeared almost catatonic, apart from the still clasping and unclasping hands. He wasn't fit to go anywhere … not even hospital. And I wasn't leaving him.

"Thanks, but no. They wouldn't let us see Pete anyway. Not tonight. We'll ring them tomorrow and find out what the situation is."

"Yes, well, maybe that's for the best," mumbled the sergeant, pulling a card out of his pocket with various police numbers printed on it. "Oh … we may need you both to make statements at some point. Just background … I appreciate you aren't exactly witnesses … as such. I've already got your contact details from Mr Holkham … how long were you planning on staying?"

"Two more nights," O'Brien said faintly but distinctly. We turned and looked at him, then the coppers looked at each other.

"According to the *Visitors' Vase*," he added.

"Yes … well …" Edwards began. "We'd best be on our way. Don't hesitate to get in touch if … well … you know …"

With that they left the warmth of the Chandlery and moments later we heard the car starting up and turning round as Steve Holkham returned with a catering-sized aluminium teapot and three enamel mugs. He filled the mugs – no milk – and then produced a bottle of rum, splashing liberal quantities into each one. I'm sure I've read somewhere you shouldn't give alcohol to people in shock, but it happens in books and clearly in real life too. In any case, I didn't feel much like challenging this local hero of positively legendary status among the saltmarshes.

Said local hero finished his tea and withdrew, telling us we could stay in the Chandlery as long as we needed given the weather was so foul. "Feel free to kip on the sailbags!" he told us, but I assured him we'd be okay aboard *Samphire* once we'd had a few more cups of tea.

"Well, I'll be at the *Bay* if you need me," he said. "Let yourselves out when you're ready; just push the doors to behind you. Oh … and feel free to take the rum. You can always drink it out of the *Visitor's Vase!*"

Half way down his second mug, O'Brien started to come round but he still had the look of a devastated soul. He closed his eyes tightly and bit his lip. His face creased into an image of inner agony no sculptor could ever replicate in marble or bronze. Then he opened his mouth and gasped repeatedly … words forming within but not emerging. Another gulp of rum-laced tea seemed to help.

"Never me!" he suddenly cried out in terrible anguish. "It's never me!"

"What isn't?" I asked, as gently as my own shredded nerves would allow.

"Never me …" he repeated, faintly this time.

I waited.

"The others. All the time it's the others."

"What others?" I coaxed.

"All of them. Julia; her family. The child. And now Peter."

"But *not* you?" I asked, beginning to understand.

"Never me!" he gasped again. "Everything I touch turns to shit.

Everyone I care for I destroy but I never suffer the consequences myself. I never … pay … for … my … sins."

"You haven't destroyed *me*," I offered.

"*Yet!*" he responded darkly, but even as he spoke I thought I could detect a flicker – the faintest scintilla perhaps – of his old ironic humour.

It was soon gone, though, as he became convulsed with great body-racking sobs. For somebody who never suffered he was making a pretty ham-fisted attempt at happiness. I almost said as much but thought better of it.

"Peter!" he groaned. "I sent him back for the petrol."

"No. He volunteered."

"But I forgot to bring it when we left Turnham …"

"We *all* forgot it," I said, trying to go down the collective responsibility line.

"If I hadn't invited you both …"

"Stop it!" I shouted. "You'll be telling me next that none of this would have happened if you hadn't been born!"

"Well at least being born wasn't my own fault!" he snapped, rallying suddenly. "But it *is* my fault the child was born. You've worked that one out, I suppose."

"Yes," I said softly. "Yes I have. There was no rape, was there?"

"No. I dealt with the bastard just in time."

Which pretty much confirmed that he was Graham's father.

"Want to tell me about it?" I asked.

"On the boat," he said. "There's something I want to show you."

We stepped out into the howling darkness, clinging on to each other as we teetered against the gale (and the rum) towards the tender. In spite of the conditions, I noticed we had a new neighbour; a big white catamaran was riding to the next buoy down the creek, a lamp burning in her ample saloon with perhaps two figures moving about in dumb-show against the curtains. Somehow we managed the short crossing and clambered over *Samphire's* rail. Once below, I lit the Tilley lamp and hung it over the table, its defiant hiss somehow comforting in its contrast with the rising wind and drumming rain. In so small a space, it was an effective provider of heat as well as light and we soon had the proverbial small-boat sailors' *fug up*. I placed the rum bottle under the lamp.

"You've got something to show me," I reminded him.

By way of an answer he produced a screwdriver from somewhere and bent down. Moments later he'd removed a bilge board and was groping in the damp cavity beneath. And there it was: a large plastic sandwich box sealed with several layers of waterproof tape. He lifted it out, gave it a wipe with a piece of old towelling and placed it on the table.

"Open it," he said, pulling a rusty jack knife from his pocket and handing it to me.

Unfolding the knife, I slid the surprisingly sharp blade into the tape and freed the lid. Inside was a self-sealing clear plastic wallet stuffed with banknotes. A lot of banknotes.

"Count it," he said.

There were 250 of them: twenties. So £5,000 in total. Not a fortune, perhaps, but almost enough to buy a small terraced house in an unpopular town.

"It's all I have left after the book deal and buying the boat," he said. "It's for the kid, now. For Graham."

"You're going to have to tell me how much of those newspaper stories – and everything else you've told me - is true," I said gravely. "No fudging this time. I want the *whole* truth. Now."

And rather to my surprise he did tell me.

The bones of the story were correct, he insisted. He had indeed found the billhook and the sacking in the hut and dressed up as Old Snetty, with the intention of reigniting the legend and monitoring the consequences. His contact with Julia Whitfield, however, had been rather more protracted. He'd actually met her in the village Post Office during the previous week, quite early in his solitary exploration of the locale. They'd got chatting and she'd offered to show him around a bit. In fact it was she who had introduced him to the hut, explaining that she sometimes met friends there to smoke dope and generally hang out.

"But we've got it to ourselves now," she'd said. Her mates were all away on holidays of their own.

And so she'd shown him the sights of Lingstead and Peddersley and the surrounding countryside; shyly distanced from each other to begin with but soon holding hands as they strolled through the waist high corn. In the heat of the hut, chaste kisses had become passionate, face-chewing embraces and – a few days into the second week – they'd finally *done it* … to use the politer teenage phraseology of the time. He was adamant the desire had been mutual. Neither had coerced or led the other on. Even so, he admitted, they had gone further than either had initially intended. So no contraception.

"And how old did you say you were?" I checked.

"We were both sixteen."

Of course. That strange limbo between childhood and adulthood when you're old enough to fight and die for your country but can't vote for how it's to be governed. Sixteen to eighteen - or was it still twenty-one back then? You could get married but couldn't watch an x rated movie! Marriage, of course, required parental consent. I wasn't sure about sex outside marriage, but I didn't imagine many teenagers got round to asking their parents' permission to *do it* … then or since!

But it hadn't been rape. At least I didn't think it was.

"So what about the attacker?" I asked. "Was he for real?"

"Yes … and no," O'Brien said, slowly resuming his infuriatingly enigmatic persona.

I sighed and held out my hands, palms uppermost.

"There was no motorist with a blue sports car," he said quickly.

"And?"

"But Julia *was* attacked. By a tramp. At least I think he was a tramp."

"Please explain."

"It was the afternoon we made love. Afterwards we shared a joint and we talked about my plans to impersonate Old Snetty. They were already well advanced by then: in fact she'd helped me with the costume so I was ready to roll. Perhaps it was the weed that gave me the final impetus … I don't know. Anyway, armed with the billhook on the pole I walked down to the lane and hid in the bushes.

"Julia opted to stay in the hut. After all, it was imperative that any potential witnesses saw only the *ghost*, so to speak … not a living sidekick! Especially one they might recognize. In half an hour or so only three cars passed. I ran across the road in front of one; alongside another for a moment; and behind the third. I was certain the first one saw me because it swerved a bit just as I leapt out of its path onto the opposite verge. The other two seemed oblivious. Still, it felt like a good start, and I hiked back up the side of the wood. *That* was when I heard Julia screaming.

"Running into the hut I found her pinned against the wall by a wild figure even scruffier than I was. Yelling furiously, I saw him off with the billhook. Julia was unharmed but obviously in serious shock. I did my best to calm her down … which required another joint or two … and the rest is pretty much as I told you before."

It took me a while to digest all this, but I decided it was no less probable – or no more improbable for that matter - than his original version.

"But why did you invent the bloke with the blue car?" I asked. "You had a real culprit. The tramp."

"Forensics were pretty advanced even then," said O'Brien. "If they'd caught him they'd know his blood group, and if Julia was pregnant with *my* child – and my blood group was different from his – they'd know he couldn't have been the father. Also, if we'd admitted she'd been attacked by a really scruffy tramp, there was a risk that I'd become a suspect myself … especially if one of those motorists really had seen me in Old Snetty mode near the wood at the material time."

It was all logical enough, I supposed. They'd needed a blind alley for the police to run up so they'd created one. Of course they couldn't have known at the time that Julia would be pregnant, but there had to be a plausible explanation if she were!

Of course there was an alternative solution …

"You obviously liked each other," I said.

"Obviously."

"You could have made an honest woman of her."

"What … married her?"

"Yes."

I was expecting him to laugh or tell me not to be so stupid, but he went very quiet again for a moment. Then, taking a swig from the rum bottle which neither of us had touched since we'd left the Chandlery, he smiled thinly.

"Do you know?" he said. "We actually talked about that. Her parents and mine might even have agreed. Catholic my side … *Anglo* Catholic hers. All very conservative … with a small *c*, anyway."

"Preferable to abortion," I remarked.

"Oh yes. None of us would have sanctioned that."

Not for the first time, it struck me as curious how some deeds are almost always regarded as sinful in certain circles and others less so … despite equal degrees of proscription. Neither the O'Briens nor the Whitfields would have countenanced abortion, but Michael and Julia had lied through their teeth about what had happened that sweltering afternoon in the hut, and in doing so had aided and abetted the escape of her attacker … the real tramp as opposed to the non-existent motorist. Either way, they had at least been guilty of obstructing a criminal investigation and wasting police time. To say nothing of pre-marital sex! It was hardly a crime these days, unless under age, yet surely anathema to good Catholics like them.

But I tried not to be judgemental. I hadn't been there, and they were only kids at the time.

Then I picked up the bag of money.

"This was a nice idea," I said. "But forget it. From what we can tell your child is well cared for and probably in a state of blissful ignorance as all children should be. Give him this and you'll raise an ugly ghost. Besides, you can't pay for what happened with mere cash."

It also crossed my mind that he'd already given Graham the priceless gift of life itself. How could £5,000 improve on that?

"It was to be anonymous," he said. I was going to land at the back of the island in the dinghy … that's what Pete's survey work was all about. Then I'd find the cottage and leave it on the doorstep and slip away. I've got to do something for my child."

"You still can," I said. "Leave him alone. Give the money to a children's charity … or the village school or something."

"I have to make amends," he groaned. "Directly. *At source*, so to speak."

"Look," I said at length. "What you did ten years ago *may* have been unlawful and was doubtless immoral – from a Catholic perspective at least – but it wasn't rape and … as far as I know, Julia's death doesn't make you a murderer. You didn't mean to cause it. I don't think it could even be construed as manslaughter."

"But she died just the same," he grunted bitterly.

"Yes. I know," I said quietly, aware now that I had perhaps skated over the heart of the tragedy a little too lightly. "And nothing will assuage the awfulness of that for those who loved her."

"*I* loved her!" he wailed.

"You most of all," I said. "But life goes on. And right now it's *Pete's* life going on I'm most concerned about. We should turn in and get some sleep before phoning the hospital first thing."

"I'll do that," he said. "I got him involved, after all. It's the least I can do."

It was a fair point, but I wasn't sure he'd be in any state to make such a call. In any case, I was pretty confident that the rapport I'd built up with Pete over the past week was stronger than O'Brien's. Not that I'd be likely to talk to Pete himself of course, but at least I could legitimately tell whoever I did speak to that I was a friend.

He nodded miserably and hauled himself out of the saloon, dragging the rum bottle with him. I crawled into my sleeping bag and lay there listening to the creak of *Samphire's* mast as it whipped about in the wind.

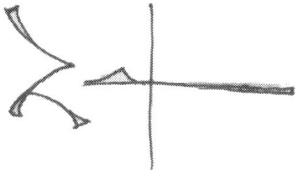

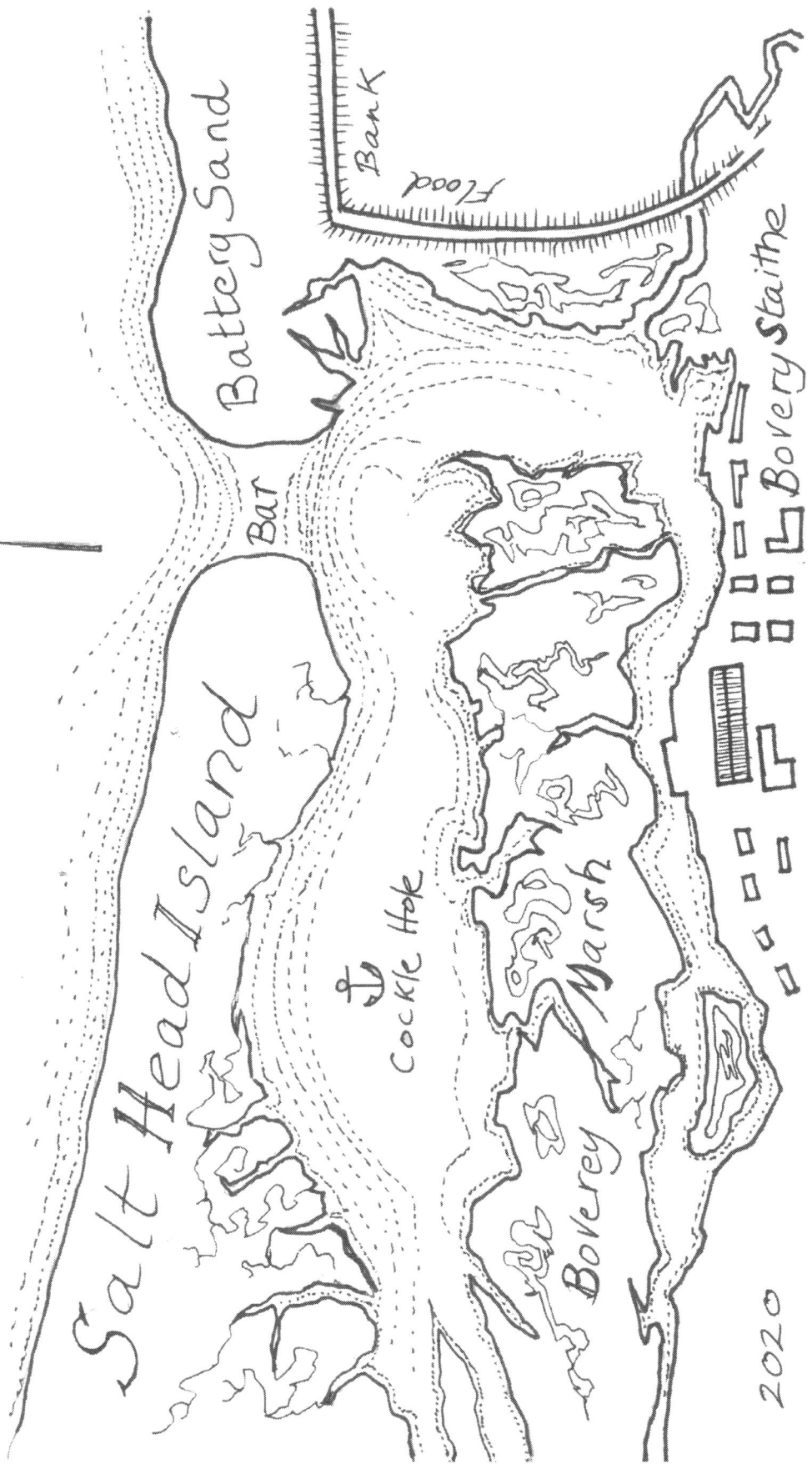

Salt Head Island

Battery Sand

Flood Bank

Bar

Cockle Hole

Bovery Staithe

Marsh

Bovery

2020

N

TEN

It was still blowing hard on Sunday morning, but the rain had eased and there were blue patches between the ragged, racing clouds. Steady snoring resonated from O'Brien's cabin and I knew there was little chance of getting him to the phone box in the village any time soon, so I scribbled him a note and rowed ashore in the tender. It was only as I was striding past the Old Chandlery that I realized I had no idea where the telephone box was … or even if there was one. Anyway, I turned right, up the lane towards the *Aboukir Bay*.

I could hear a tinny rattle even over the racket of the wind and saw Steve Holkham rolling empty metal kegs into a corner of the yard. No doubt he'd be able to direct me to a phone so I gave him a shout and a wave.

"Don't be daft!" he called back. "Come on in and use mine!"

He led me into the kitchen via the back door and pointed to a venerable Bakelite instrument on the sideboard. It had a proper chrome dial as opposed to the increasingly ubiquitous buttons and there was something comforting about it. Perhaps it was simply the relief that I wouldn't have to keep feeding a limited supply of coins into a slot during a conversation of un-guessable duration. Holkham also knew the hospital's number by heart: I suppose that went with the territory of being a Voluntary Coastguard.

As I started to dial, he began piling rashers of bacon into a blackened skillet on the big range and cracking eggs into a bowl.

Rather as I had anticipated, I had quite a struggle convincing a sequence of telephonists that I was a fit and proper person to be enquiring about a patient, and it was only when I referred the third or fourth intermediary to the local constabulary's records of the accident that they started to relent. Papers were shuffled; shoes squeaked on lino; doors opened and closed and other phones were lifted and replaced, but eventually I was put through to the Sister in charge of Peter's ward, who was the absolute embodiment of helpful reassurance.

In short … her news was good. Peter had broken a lot of bones but –

despite having been launched headlong through the taxi's windscreen – his skull remained mercifully intact. He was still in a coma, but assorted scanning techniques appeared to show fairly normal brain activity and it was felt that he stood a reasonable chance of a full mental recovery. His spinal column was battered but unbroken and although a return to full mobility was certainly possible, this was likely to take quite some time. The probability was that if and when full consciousness was regained, he would be moved to a long-term special mobility unit on the outskirts of Norwich. I was welcome to visit the hospital but warned that there was probably little point just at the moment.

I gave her my home phone number and address, thanked her sincerely and rang off.

Steve Holkham wouldn't accept any cash for the call and gestured towards the plate of bacon and scrambled egg he'd just set down on the scrubbed deal table.

"For me?"

"Of course. Even if you've breakfasted already a second one won't do you any harm on a day like today. What about your mate? Mike, I mean."

"Dead to the world," I said, sitting down and picking up the cutlery.

"Not surprised," he chuckled. "Good stuff, that rum!"

*

When I'd finished this very welcome repast and begun my return to the boat, I discovered the rain had come back with a vengeance. The patches of blue sky had gone too, the ragged clouds having coagulated back into a leaden pall.

Something else which had gone was the boat.

I reached the tender pulled up on the grass and stood staring at the empty sheet of rain-spattered water where *Samphire* had been. My first thought was that she'd parted her cable in the blow and drifted off down the creek with her skipper still out for the count. I quickly scanned the waterway downwind but there was no sign of her: surely she'd have snagged one of the other craft … not least the shiny new catamaran which had appeared next door. They were all tugging at their moorings but none appeared tangled up with an errant old lugger.

Samphire really had gone.

There was a shout from the catamaran and I squinted through the slanting shafts of rain at a blurred figure emerging onto her broad afterdeck. He appeared to be holding up a bundle of some sort which I suddenly realised was my rucksack. Cupping my hands around my ears to catch his message I eventually made out the words: "Your mate asked me to give you this. Taking a bit of a risk, isn't he?" I could also make out he name of his craft: *Cat-Astrophe*.

I shoved the tender into the water and scrambled aboard, rowing out to the white cat. Her owner took the painter and made fast to cleat on the deck.

"You saw him go?" I asked.

"Ten minutes ago. Shipping forecast's giving out a gale warning. I did tell him but he insisted."

Once again I regretted having not bought a radio when we'd had the chance.

"Under sail?" I asked, hauling myself – uninvited – up onto *Cat-Astrophe's* afterdeck.

"He was just starting to hoist his canvas when I spotted him. I'm Jake, by the way. Jake Carter."

"Evan," I said, shaking his hand … absurdly formal under the circumstances. He was a stocky, barrel-chested chap in his early forties with a sandy fringe, but quite athletic-looking for all his bulk.

He said, "I shouted across that he'd be safer under his engine given the forecast. Said he was out fuel so I threw him a line and sent him a can-full since he wasn't going beyond the sand bar."

"Is that what he told you?" I asked.

"Why?" asked the putative Good Samaritan, looking somewhat alarmed now.

"Any reason to doubt him?"

"I'm not sure," I said hesitantly, shaking my head and thinking hard.

"Come below, man!" he entreated. "Out of the wind for God's sake!"

I followed him through the companionway and down into the wide saloon suspended between the twin hulls. I've always felt that catamarans resemble aircraft rather than boats, with a flight deck sung between the wings. For'ard, two deeply padded swivel chairs faced an elaborate instrument panel and comfortable banquettes lined the remaining bulkheads. I guessed the sleeping berths were tucked away in the twin hulls. A neat pile of distinctly feminine clothing lay on one of the banquettes, so I'd been right about seeing two figures last night.

"So he told you he was just going to the lagoon?" I asked again.

"Well … yes," replied Jake. "Implied it, anyway. Something about a house on the island? I didn't know there was one."

My rucksack seemed heavier than I remembered, so I undid the flap and peered inside. The first thing I saw was the bag of money. So he'd given up on that idea, then.

"Did he say anything else?" I asked.

"No. Er … yes! I mean he gave me a letter to post. Somewhere on the Welsh border, I think. Name of Price."

"That's me."

"But I could have given it you myself," said Jake, frowning.

"You still could."

"No. Maggie – that's my wife – rowed ashore for the Sunday papers twenty minutes ago. She took it to post." He glanced at the bulkhead clock. "It'll be in the box by now."

I slumped onto one of the deep blue velveteen banquettes.

"Something's wrong, isn't it?" he said.

"Something's very wrong," I replied softly.

If Michael were heading for the bird warden's cottage, he surely would have taken the money with him, but he knew – or at least I *think* he knew – that it was too far up the lagoon to approach in a vessel such as *Samphire*, even with her centreboard retracted. That was the principal explanation for the dinghy and Peter's meticulous chartwork. Of course he might have been planning to run ashore on the lagoon beach and walk to the cottage. But that left the matter of the money. Surely the whole point of this entire operation had been to deliver the cash to the Sykes' doorstep.

I now knew he wasn't heading for their cottage. In fact he wasn't heading for the island at all.

I relayed a doubtless garbled version of all this to Jake, concluding by saying we needed to put to sea immediately if there was any hope of saving O'Brien.

Jake nodded but said we'd have to wait until Maggie got back. Meanwhile, he'd alert the lifeboat and coastguard.

"Steve Holkham?"

"No. Hunswick. They'll alert Steve anyway."

Even as he reached for a radio mic on the instrument console there was a bumping along the starboard hull and Maggie was climbing aboard. She was about the same age as her husband but slimmer, with an unruly mop of slightly greying curls roughly tied back with a red ribbon. She stopped and stared at Jake, listening intently for a moment. Then she spotted me and did a kind of double take.

Jake signed off and made speedy introductions.

"Forecast's terrible," he said. "But I'm prepared to take her over the bar and hover around until the lifeboat arrives."

"No need," I said hastily. "Do you have a hand-held VHF and a pair of binos?" (I'd left mine aboard *Samphire*.)

He nodded.

"Just take me up to the bar and drop me at the Battery Sand end. I can jump ashore and have a look out from the dunes. You can search the lagoon in case I'm wrong. What's she draw?"

"Three feet max at the rudders," said Maggie. "But what the heck's going on?"

"Mercy mission," her husband responded. "Tell you on the way."

He tossed me a radio in a waterproof pouch and a heavily rubberised pair of glasses before pressing a switch which fired up the big outboard mounted between the twin hulls aft. Compared with *Samphire's* rattly little *Seagull* it sounded like a high performance racing car even in neutral. Maggie jumped back through the companionway, skipped round the side deck onto the for'ard netting and slipped the cable to the buoy, leaving both tenders attached to it. *Cat-Astrophe* spun in her own length and moved off down the creek, carefully keeping to the channel between the mooring lines and the marsh opposite the hard.

We reached the first bend and turned northwards. A few more boats were moored ahead of us, but there was nothing immediately visible in the lagoon which gradually opened up to port. The marshes had turned a dirty brown and even the relatively sheltered water behind the island was alive with coffee coloured spume. Ahead, beyond the bar, the ocean itself seemed to stand up like a black and trembling wall. The bar itself was already covered and there was no sign of *Samphire* on either side of it.

We edged as near as we dared to the line of foam delineating the presence of the bar beneath. Jake didn't say anything but I guessed he was feeling considerable relief at not being obliged to cross it. Catamarans may offer luxury undreamed of in mono-hulls, but if they tip over they can be a devil to right; especially big ones like this.

"Get her up to that beach," I said, pointing to a small crescent of sand scooped out the floodbank on our starboard bow. "I'll jump and you can back off when I'm clear."

He nodded and adjusted our course slightly to the east. I stuffed the new equipment into my rucksack and slung it over one shoulder. "Be careful!" called Maggie as I left the saloon.

Once on the for'ard netting I realised I'd have either to climb over - or duck under - the pulpit rail. Given *Cat-Astrophe's* motion I wanted to keep my centre of gravity as low as possible until the actual moment of the jump, so ducking under looked like the safer option. I made my way out onto the prow of the starboard hull and braced myself into the pulpit. I heard the engine throttle back to slow ahead but we had the wind with us and the bank was rushing towards me.

No time for hesitation.

I slipped the rucksack down to my right hand and whirled it over my shoulder, sending it cart-wheeling over the spray. Dropping under the rail in almost the same fluid movement, I drove both feet hard against the gunwale and launched myself over the three or four feet of intervening foam with only my boots in the water. To my utter astonishment I cleared the gap and belly-flopped into the soft sand. Rolling over and looking back, I saw *Cat-Astrophe* had got off safely and was turning round to shudder crabwise over the mounting swell. I waved vigorously to show that I was alright and struggled to my feet in search of my rucksack.

I found it quickly and scrambled up the floodbank, turning along the path towards the big dune known locally as Battery Sand. (Presumably it had at one time mounted a gun emplacement of some kind, though nobody knew exactly when or why.) Rough, tussocky hillocks appeared on both sides of the path now as it turned sharply to the east. At this point I carried straight on, slithering down the bank into a saucer of marram, flattened by the driving wind. Directly ahead, the biggest sand hill of all rose like mountain, with a rough track zig-zagging up its flank. In places, this track had been reinforced with duckboards but these were mostly buried or missing. It was a taxing climb and I had to keep turning into the wind to refill my lungs.

The summit commanded an endless panorama of writhing water: grey-green sickle-shaped sweeps of brine harvesting the beaches, laced with smoking fringes of snow-white spray. The German Ocean, they used to call it, in less patriotic times before the World Wars. Incredible to think it was the same sea we'd traversed all the way round from King's Lynn, and where we'd run out of petrol a couple of miles further out. My memory had made a placid lake of it, but this was a real ocean now. As the locals never tired of telling visitors: look north and there's no land until the Arctic ice; look east and there are no hills until the Urals.

I pulled out the binos and swept the horizon to and fro, sometimes lowering the lenses a little to check I wasn't missing anything important closer in. But there was nothing. Once I thought I glimpsed a speck of a tan-bark sail in the middle distance but it was only a gull rolling boisterously on the wind, its juvenile plumage contrasting with the white spume beneath it. The horizon itself was disappearing now: there could have been a supertanker out there and I wouldn't have seen it in the flying scud. I radioed *Cat-Astrophe* and told Jake I'd drawn a blank. He said they'd run westwards along the back of the island until their echo sounder started bleeping shrill warnings, but they'd seen no vessel of any kind on the lagoon.

Switching to channel nine I picked up Coastguard and RNLI chatter straight away. I joined in the conversation, stating my position and explaining what I could - or rather *couldn't* - see from my vantage point. Somebody asked for a description of *Samphire* and when I'd given it I thought I heard another voice crackle: "Not a bloody hope!" I probably wasn't meant to hear that bit.

Moments later the Hunswick Lifeboat hove into view, bouncing over the rollers and sending up swan's wings of spray from her bows. It was the proper one, with big diesel inboards and a cabin … not the inshore RIB I'd been anticipating. Somebody mentioned a helicopter and I looked around for a yellow Sea King, fancying I could hear rotors thumping through the cloud base. Nothing materialized, however. Perhaps it was further out, obscured by spray and scud.

I called Jake again and told him I was heading back for Boverey. Turning my back on the sea, I began lurching down the sliding sand of the slope towards the path along the flood bank. Half way back to the Staithe I saw a sturdy wooden motorboat batting down the creek towards me. Steve Holkham was at the wheel and I waved as he passed but he didn't seem to notice; he was locked into full professional mode now, gripping the spokes and staring intently ahead.

It seemed like a long slog back to the Staithe, but of course I'd been up half the night and had been hard at it since dawn. When I eventually staggered into the village, the Old Chandlery was locked and of course the pub wasn't yet open, especially considering the landlord was now exercising one of his many alternative roles. I couldn't think of any other premises which might be open except the church … it was Sunday after all. But the church was mile or two further inland and I was close to collapse.

Once again, however, *Cat-Astrophe* proved my refuge. She was back on her mooring and Jake – whom I suspect had been keeping an eye out for my return – came rowing over to pick me up.

"We're here for a few days," he said. "Feel free to kip on board."

It turned out that the twin hulls were long enough to house two berths each. Jake and Maggie slept head-to-toe to starboard whilst the port berths were currently used for stowage of gear. A bit of judicious re-stowing, however, cleared the forward berth which meant the saloon could remain clear.

They knocked up a simple lunch and left the VHF on channel nine so we could monitor the remainder of the search for *Samphire*. There was even an RAF Nimrod involved now: she'd been on routine patrol off the Firth of Forth and was diverted south but had spotted nothing. As Jake pointed out, the half can of petrol he'd given Mike would surely have run out by now and a boat as small as his would be having a really hard time in ever worsening conditions. Even *Cat-Astrophe* would have struggled.

"Just how experienced is your friend?" asked Maggie.

"Hardly at all, I'm afraid," I said. "Me neither."

"Then what …" she began but her husband held up a hand.

"I will explain," I yawned. "But I'd like to sleep first."

"Of course!" they chimed in unison and I crawled gratefully into *Cat-Astrophe's* port hull.

*

The following day I set out on the first stage of my homeward journey, taking the bus to King's Lynn where I booked into a shabby but comfortable hotel for one night. It overlooked Tuesday Market, that great sea of cobbles which I felt was crying out for some kind of mass protest of Mitteleuropean peasantry just waiting to be cut down by Cossacks or flamboyant hussars. Quite why, I don't know. Perhaps it was just my sombre mood.

I did visit the hospital – my main reason for stopping here - and was allowed to look at Peter through a glazed door. He was still in a coma but the prognosis remained reasonably hopeful. I enquired if his parents were in Lynn and was surprised to discover that they were staying in the same hotel as myself. I may have seen them already, but of course I wouldn't have recognised them.

Nor they me.

On my return to the hotel it was tempting to avoid eye-contact with any middle aged couples I chanced upon … just in case. Although my own conscience was entirely clear, they weren't to know I hadn't been instrumental in luring their son into this mad escapade which might have cost him his life. In the event, however, there was only one middle aged couple staying there and I felt I had no choice but to approach them in the bar. I needn't have worried. Ashen with anxiety though they were, they seemed to take the view that any friend of Peter's was a friend of theirs. They insisted I had dinner with them that night and I was able to fill them in on so much they didn't know. Mr Rufford had a silver goatee and gold-rimmed half-moon specs: I thought he looked like an Am Dram society's idea of a police surgeon or country solicitor. Mrs Rufford somehow preserved a cheerful demeanour in spite of everything. Nice people.

When I explained that our vehicles were both still at Bradwell St Helen, Mr Rufford immediately offered to drive me there tomorrow morning so I could rescue my own, and he could make arrangements for the recovery of his son's Mini.

And so he did. While Mrs Rufford kept watch at the hospital, her husband took me to Bradwell in his silver Capri. The weather was improving again and a journey which had effectively taken a couple of days aboard *Samphire* was accomplished in just over an hour. We were crunching over the gravel in front of *the Six Horseshoes* shortly before lunchtime opening.

Mr Sherriff seemed quite unsurprised to see us, despite never having set eyes on Peter's father before. We ordered a couple of cheese and pickle rolls and a pint of bitter each and chose not to go into any detail about the accident. However, the landlord brought both sets of car keys on the tray with our pints and Mr Rufford found himself having to summarize the situation in order to explain that he couldn't drive both his Capri and his son's Mini at the same time.

"I was hoping to find someone to deliver it for me," he said.

Sherriff nodded sagely and informed him that there was an excellent haulier in Walpole Highway with all the right gear. "My cousin," he added. "I'll give him a ring. Oh … and it'll be family rates, of course."

Of course.

After lunch Peter's father and myself parted company, having exchanged contact details and promising to keep in touch. I said how much I hoped his son would make a complete recovery. He nodded solemnly as he climbed into his Capri and gave me a slow wave as he drove off towards Lynn. There was a lump in my throat as I turned the old Morris westwards towards that other world I'd left seemingly a lifetime ago. By now the harvest was mostly complete and the stubble shone – if anything – even whiter than the grain that had gone. In places it was being burned back, and palls of grey-brown smoke drifted along the implacable horizons like tokens of distant warfare.

Four and a half hours later I pulled up outside the somewhat neglected Edwardian villa which housed my bachelor bedsit in the outskirts of Hay-on-Wye. Sure enough, Michael O'Brien's letter was waiting for me on the dusty table in the communal hallway. Naturally, reading it was top priority … along with pouring myself a tumbler of scotch.

Collapsing into a lumpy old armchair by the empty grate, I took a pull at the scotch, set down the glass on the tiled hearth and contemplated the envelope in my lap. My name and address were smudged: of course it had been raining in Boverey Staithe when Maggie Carter had taken it to the post box. I tore open the slightly cockled envelope.

Unlike his previous communications with Peter and myself, this one was hand-written … for obvious reasons. But the style – the very *feel* of it – was much the same:-

Even at the very end I didn't tell you everything. But you do deserve to know the whole truth now. Tell them to dig behind the hut. That will explain all, I think.

I am deeply grateful to both of you for all you did to help me in my crazy enterprise. To be honest, I think all I really needed was an audience and you certainly provided one; so thanks again. If – God willing – Pete pulls through, do make sure to tell him so with my gratitude.

The money is yours if you want it. If not, throw it in the sea.

Michael

I drained my glass and re-read the letter. It told me everything and nothing.

EPILOGUE

A Coroner's jurisdiction is said to end at the low water mark.

From time to time, however, a Coroner with responsibility for a coastal region will find himself facing something of a legal conundrum. When somebody dies – or is *thought* to have died – at sea, with evidence that they had last been seen alive on *terra firma* within his particular area of jurisdiction, it *may* be claimed in law that the fatality had occurred **near** his area, in which case it *might* be appropriate to hold an inquest. If, however, said fatality (or putative fatality) can be shown to have taken place outside the three mile territorial limit, then no such inquest can take place. *Even where a crime is suspected.*

Herein lies the difficulty.

The nature of tidal action is such that a body found floating, or dredged from the seabed, beyond the three mile limit may have originated within it (thus allowing for at least the possibility of an inquest) but a body discovered within said limit may have originated beyond it … thus *precluding* any possibility of such an inquest!

Where there is no body – but every reason to believe that there *should* be one – these complexities are multiplied one hundred-fold. In such circumstances, an inquest is rarely, if ever, held … perhaps because no Coroner would actually have the patience (or even the ability) to determine whether to hold one would be strictly legal within the meaning of the act.

Thus it was with the disappearance of Michael O'Brien.

His body was never found, but *Samphire's* mast (or a spar very much like it) had come ashore at Flatte, on the extreme eastern end of the great saltmarsh, where ramparts of shingle take over from sand and sedge. A dozen or so tins of baked beans had been found between Chesterfleet and Wakeney and the splintered remains of what may have been *Samphire's* sliding doghouse were cast up near Cokeham Pumps.

Ironically, though, the process by which it had been determined *not* to hold an inquest had involved the hearing of evidence from so many sources – such as the Police; Coastguard; RNLI and the Marine Accident

Investigation Unit; to say nothing of individuals such as myself, Steve Holkham and the Carters - that it dragged on for days and ultimately proved itself to be an inquest *de facto* if not *de jure*. There was no jury or verdict of course, but a concluding statement was prepared and read out by a local aristocrat rejoicing in the splendidly arcane title of *General-at-Sea on the Saxon Shore*. He wore a comic opera uniform with plenty of gold lace, and carried a ceremonial silver-plated oar over his shoulder.

His proclamation told us exactly we already knew.

Michael O'Brien had almost certainly drowned when his boat *Samphire* had foundered somewhere north or north east of Boverey Staithe. Said drowning may or may not have been intentional. His final letter to me was not held specific enough to constitute a suicide note.

With regard to the traffic accident which had killed two drivers and injured Peter Rufford so drastically, the cause was so obviously the recklessness of the driver of the Ford Escort that an inquest was likewise deemed unnecessary. Peter, who was now able to speak coherently (though as yet unable to walk unaided) had given an account which more or less corroborated the statements of others and matched the forensic analysis undertaken by the Traffic Division. Unsurprisingly, he could not recall the moment of impact, but his last memory was indeed of a pair of headlights looming towards him at speed on the wrong side of the road.

*

When it came to the grim discovery behind the shed in the wood, however, a proper inquest looked increasingly likely. Naturally I was required to give a considerable amount of evidence and it made sense to decamp to Hunswick for duration. Remarkably, my editor was still in a generous mood regarding leave, but he obviously felt there was something in it for him. Clearly there was a potential scoop here, but it had precious little to do with the Welsh Marches! I supposed he may have envisaged basking in the reflected glory of my *story about a story* when it eventually hit the nationals, and take credit for it as my mentor.

Anyway, in mid February I booked into the *Golden Griffin* and even secured a room with a sea view. It was only when I looked out of the window that I realised the pier had now vanished entirely! The East Coast had certainly taken a battering over the winter.

The inquest itself was held in a rather bleak public hall of some sort behind the Tourist Information Office; one of those places which always seem to smell of dust and disinfectant. Peter had now been transferred to the specialist mobility unit near Norwich and was making real progress. He was even walking short distances with a frame, but a nurse was in constant attendance just in case he started to wobble. I managed to visit him two or three times on the days when I wasn't required to give evidence myself. He was keen to make the trip to Hunswick if at all practicable, but the Coroner had declared tape-recorded interviews with Peter to be admissible so long as they were properly certified as genuine. I think Pete was a little disappointed by this as boredom was taking its toll. On the other hand, I rather got the impression that he was starting to find at least one of the nursing staff there quite the opposite of boring!

Naturally I had already accompanied the police forensics team, along with a couple of lady archaeologists from the University of East Anglia, to the wood near Lingstead. It struck me, as we walked up the path from the lane, that I hadn't actually visited the hut itself; I just *knew* where it was from O'Brien's accounts of it. In reality, though, the hut itself had more or less disappeared after a decade of summer growth and winter storms, but there were still sufficient sheets of corrugated iron and rotten planks lying amongst the brambles to indicate roughly where it had stood. The police were dubious at first, but the archaeologists seemed to have a sixth sense about these things. They quickly located the line of the back wall and were thus able to determine what *behind* it meant. Then, once they'd hacked back the shrubbery, one of them pointed at the obviously disturbed earth beneath.

"Could be foxes," she said. "In which case we might not find much."

"True," said her companion. "But you'd think if foxes had been unearthing body parts and dumping them all over the landscape someone might have noticed!"

The supervising DI shook his head: "You'd be surprised at what *doesn't* get noticed, especially in wooded terrain. We found a severed head once … *up a tree … in a public park,* would you believe!"

"Well at least foxes don't normally climb trees," replied the girl, kneeling down and starting to trowel the soil aside carefully.

Before they found the bones they found the billhook, or what was left of it - a paper-thin sliver of flaky rust with the slightly thicker remains of a socket at one end. The wooden shaft was just a stain in the soil. Though it had probably been made in my lifetime (or not long before) the two archaeologists treated it with the care they'd give to an Iron Age sword or – indeed – a genuinely medieval relic of the Peasants' Revolt. It was over half an hour before they had it clear of the earth and into a plastic box, carefully padded and supported with bubble wrap and expanded polystyrene chips. One of them had a quality SLR and took numerous photographs of each phase of the operation. The Police took pictures of their own.

The first bone turned up almost an hour later. It was a long bone and probably human. The second was unmistakable: a human pelvis. There was no attempt to remove the skeleton; only to expose as much of it as had survived.

Which was most of it.

A handful of smaller bones was indeed missing. Doubtless they lay in a fox's earth somewhere … or just in the undergrowth, pecked clean by crows; gnawed by rats. They were not the kind anyone other than an expert would necessary recognise as human.

I think we all gasped when we saw the skull. Skulls are always shocking of course, largely because of the rather trashy way we use them as images of horror or warnings of danger. But archaeologists and policemen are inured to that kind of thing. This time, the real shock was the deep cleft in the bone, a clean slice from over the right ear to the left eye socket. It would need an expert to confirm it of course, but it was obvious to all of us that the billhook had been responsible. Or rather … the person wielding it.

"Okay, we'll call it a day for now," said the DI. "We'll secure the site and get Uniform to mount a guard."

"And call Dr Bentley?" asked one of his juniors.

"No, lad. This chap's been dead a long time. Dr Bentley can have a night in for once and submit his two penn'th come the inquest."

Another officer pulled a roll of plastic sheeting from his backpack and they began pegging it out over the shallow grave. Clearly Michael O'Brien's account of that long-ago summer was going to have to be adjusted one more time, only now he wasn't around to make the adjustments himself. That would be up to the Coroner's jury … God help them!

*

Coroner's inquests seem to be pretty much a law unto themselves. Apparently there is little requirement these days for a jury to be empanelled at all, but this case had been deemed sufficiently unusual to warrant one. Even so, the Coroner himself was not bound in law to abide by the jury's conclusions if he disagreed with them. This latter point not unnaturally triggered a general raising of eyebrows and a degree of stifled muttering across the hall. The jurors themselves, however, remained quietly attentive. I presume Mr Justice Lavenham-Burke had already apprised them of this seeming anomaly. He also explained to the whole assembly that it was no longer within the remit of anyone present at an inquest to apportion legal blame should it emerge that a crime had been committed. I suspect he had the press in mind particularly … which I found slightly sobering. After all, I had been a fairly regular occupier of the Press Gallery myself … though never at a Coroner's inquest.

Of course I could only present such evidence as I had perceived it up to the time of Michael's disappearance. The Coroner had made it quite clear that drawing conclusions from anybody's evidence was up to the jury and himself: not the witnesses.

In one sense, I had a fairly easy ride of it. I'd written and re-written so many draughts of my putative article that I had the gist of it by heart. Thus I was able to stand in the improvised witness box and deliver – even though I say so myself - a thoroughly engaging account of that weird week in late August with all its high adventure, strange discoveries and ultimate tragedy. Admittedly the Coroner reminded the members of the jury that I was a journalist by profession as soon as I'd finished. But at least he said it with a smile.

But nothing I'd said appeared to contradict anything that anybody else had said, though of course the discovery of the skeleton did *not* accord with my account of O'Brien's story, in which the tramp had run away. O'Brien's last letter, on the other hand, had made it quite clear that he hadn't been entirely straight with me even then, and that therefore my version was still an honest account *of what I had been told*.

Naturally I'd produced the bag of money as material evidence at the *non-inquest*, but it had been returned to me on the grounds that O'Brien's last letter had effectively bequeathed it to me. So it would appear that whilst it could *not* be construed as a suicide note, it *could* be regarded as a will.

A similar situation arose at the real inquest. My previous deposition (which had of course mentioned the money) was now in the public domain and I felt I had no option but to produce the cash again. The Coroner, however, made it clear to the jury that the mere fact that O'Brien had been carrying a large sum of money aboard his boat was not necessarily relevant to the matter in hand, which was simply establishing the identity and fate of the human remains discovered in Lingstead Wood. It might become relevant at a later date, he explained, if a criminal investigation ensued; in which case a forensic accountant might be retained to establish that O'Brien himself had acquired it legally.

So once again the money was returned into my keeping and I was not obliged to explain what O'Brien had been intending to do with it in anything other than the vaguest of terms. This was something of a relief as one of my chief concerns all along had been to minimise any negative impact the hearing might have upon the Whitfield family. (I didn't know it at the time, but Julia's parents were attending daily. I did, however, think I spotted brother William on one occasion, tucked away as close to the doors as possible.)

I confess I had skated over the conversation with John Hardacre at Cokeham Pumps, and I certainly didn't mention the senior moment in which he had accidentally named the adopted child. Nor did I say much about Anne Bates, simply referring to her as someone O'Brien had consulted in the course of his own investigations. If pushed further, I could truthfully say I'd neither met nor spoken to her.

William Whitfield, on the other hand, was another matter. I had undoubtedly met him, and his apparent reckless use of a firearm certainly caught the Coroner's attention. Indeed, the hearing was suspended for an afternoon whilst the local Firearms Liaison Officer paid a visit to Whitfield's tied cottage near Peddersley. It transpired, however, that the brother's only registered shotgun had been under repair with a reputable gunsmith in Swaffham at the material time. As there had never been any complaint or suspicion that Whitfield held any *unregistered* weapons, the officer had simply left him with a friendly warning to take care how he stored his ammunition: leaving boxes of cartridges on windowsills in full view of the street really wasn't such a bright idea, though apparently it was a common enough occurrence hereabouts.

So it looked as if the shots we heard may well have been fired by a poacher after all … or even just a car backfiring in the night. The figure I'd seen earlier would just have to remain a mystery, though it was reasonable to assume that he had had something to do with poachers … or even smugglers. (Dutch hand-rolling tobacco was commonly imported via the saltmarshes, apparently.)

But all this was just preliminary, of course. The public – and the press – were still waiting for the main event: the attempt to identify the bones from behind the shed, establish a cause of death and – if such a cause proved suspicious – to determine whether or not a crime had been committed: though not, of course, to name a suspect.

Establishing the victim's precise identity was always going to be difficult given the time which had elapsed and the consequent state of the remains. Dental records had come up with nothing, though there was talk of a new technique involving the analysis of tooth enamel to determine place of birth. This, however, was still in its experimental stages and prohibitively expensive. Even blood-type was proving extremely difficult to determine. The victim was certainly male and – according to Dr Bentley – had probably died in his forties or fifties. The archaeologists from UEA confirmed this assertion. Very little had been found in terms of clothing; just some fragments of seriously decayed sheepskin suggesting a coat or jacket of some kind. One fragment even had a large mock-ivory button attached, with a maker's mark stamped on the back. The mark was traced to a company which had ceased to trade in 1947.

So the coat was already over twenty years old at the time of its burial.

Likewise the footwear … or what was left of it. A few slivers of leather had been found around the feet. A spokesman for the forensics team explained that it had originally been quality material – doubtless both thick and supple – but showed signs of multiple and rather amateurish mending, as well as the effects of a decade underground. More curious was the collection of small nodules of rust – dozens of them - which had been found in the soil just below the feet. These were almost certainly hobnails, and real hobnail boots had surely passed into legend between the wars.

O'Brien had not really described what the tramp had been wearing when he attacked Julia Whitfield – at least not in any detail beyond *scruffy* and *rough* - but old and much-mended items certainly conformed to the popular notion of what a tramp was traditionally expected to look like. A social historian from Cambridge, with a particular interest in rural culture, did point out that tramps usually had regular beats which followed the cycle of seasonal labour. Often, they were on reasonable terms with the communities through which they passed and knew very well who would - and who would not - offer them a cup of tea and a few slices of bread. Or let them sleep in their barns. The failure of such a visitor to appear on cue might, she suggested, have been noticed by the charitably inclined.

"Indeed," said the Coroner politely, "but I must remind the jury that ten years have passed since the events we are considering here. I should imagine it would have been the older – dare I say more traditional - members of the community who would have been most likely to show kindness of this nature. Not wishing to be morbid, but one wonders how many of that generation remain?"

The professor conceded the point with a nod of the head, though I thought I detected the ghost of a frown as she returned to her seat. The members of the Jury were also nodding, clearly in agreement with the Coroner.

As noted previously, much of what I'd laid before the court was simply my own recollection of what O'Brien had told me. Strictly speaking, I supposed it may have been hearsay and therefore inadmissible. I could produce nothing which O'Brien had written down, except his letters to Peter and myself and – in the sterile atmosphere of a courtroom – these proved enigmatic to the point of opacity. On the other hand, Peter's recorded interview contradicted nothing I had said. The bottom line was that that the jury had got to hear our evidence whether the Coroner considered it admissible or not. If so, he seemed very relaxed about it all!

Whoever the victim actually was, there could surely have been little doubt as to how he had come by his death.

Dr Bentley submitted a sequence of photographs of the skeleton, both in its proverbial *shallow grave* and re-articulated on a table in his pathology lab. He concentrated, however, on images of the skull taken from various angles, all clearly showing the deep cleft in the bone. In the final example, the remains of the billhook had been placed in the wound. It sat neatly in the slot like a knife resting in a pat of butter. It was not, he explained, a *perfect* fit, as the blade had been marginally thicker prior to a decade of accelerated corrosion, but there was no doubt in his mind that this was at least potentially the implement which had caused the victim's death.

"Why only potentially?" asked Lavenham-Burke.

"Because whilst toxicology has revealed nothing of note, it is at least theoretically possible that he was poisoned – or even died of natural causes – and the blow struck posthumously for some reason."

"Do you think that likely, Dr Bentley?"

Bentley paused for a moment: "I think … that's not for me to say. There's absolutely nothing to suggest it, but stranger things have happened, I suppose."

A matter for the jury, then.

The Coroner nodded and turned over a sheet of paper.

"When it comes to the nature of the blow," continued the doctor, "we have already heard from Mr Price's account of O'Brien's story, that a pole had been lashed into the socket of the billhook, thus effectively converting an agricultural implement into an infantry weapon of a quasi-medieval nature. I understand this pole to have been about five feet long and I am reasonably confident that the assailant was almost certainly right-handed. I suspect that he or she will have gripped the shaft with the right hand at about the half way point, with the left hand near the foot. Approaching from behind, the attacker will have swung the weapon up above his or her right shoulder, pushed forward and down with the right hand whilst jerking back and upwards with the left, thus causing the pole to cartwheel and the blade to chop down upon the head of the victim ."

"Could such an attack have taken place within the confines of so a small hut?" asked the Coroner.

"Almost certainly not. In my view, the attacker followed him and struck the blow just outside the structure, then dragged the body round to where it was buried."

I smiled thinly. He could only have known that Michael O'Brien was right-handed because I'd probably implied it when talking about him in connection with boaty stuff. To prove his hypothesis, he would have had to have given the suspect a name, which of course none of us was allowed to do in public. His phrase *reasonably confident* got him off the hook. If there were any pathological evidence to be had from the bones which might suggest right-handedness, he didn't mention it.

"Perhaps I should add," Dr Bentley continued, "that Miss Delahaye, who is one of the archaeologists working with the forensics team, has recently worked on a mass burial near a medieval battlefield in France, and she reports many such injuries to skulls, doubtless inflicted by weapons of this type."

I wondered, just for a moment, if someone was going to raise the possibility that the burial in Lingstead Wood was a genuinely medieval inhumation; a relic, perhaps, of an incident in the Peasants' Revolt. But I suppose buttons dating from the 1940s pretty much ruled it out.

And so the Coroner, presumably satisfied that there was nothing more to be contributed by way of evidence, came to his summing up. Once again he reminded the members of the jury that – should they bring in a verdict of unlawful killing or any of its variants – this must not include any accusations levelled at named individuals, so as not to prejudice any criminal trial which might ensue. (Not that he necessarily envisaged such a trial occurring.) He explained that whilst there was nothing to suggest that the death had been accidental, a verdict of suicide was technically open to them along the lines of Dr Bentley's observation that the blow to the head could – at least theoretically – have been delivered posthumously for some unfathomable reason. He added, almost *sotto voce*, that they were entirely at liberty to dismiss this notion as unlikely to the point of absurdity if they so wished. Especially since no other cause of death had been suggested.

Both murder and manslaughter could be considered, but it was nothing short of *imperative* (he almost struck his bench on this point) to remember that – barring the existence of persons completely unknown to this court – there were only three possible witnesses to the events which had been unfolded before them … two of whom were most assuredly dead and the third *almost certainly* so.

Just before he sent them out to consider their verdict he reiterated the fact that he was not actually obliged to accept their decision as binding.

"Be assured, though," he added, "that I shall look upon the fruits of your labour with gratitude and respect."

To their credit, the jurors were out for a good three and a half hours, which presumably indicated that they were taking the case seriously and thinking things through. On their return, the foreman asked Lavenham-Burke how much commentary upon their deliberations they might be permitted to supply in order to clarify their verdict.

The Coroner ruminated for a moment, chewing his lower lip.

"Were this a criminal trial," he said at length, "I would say none at all, given that what is said in the jury room quite properly remains in the jury room for all time. However, since no-one is actually on trial here, I am minded to request that you give your verdict as concisely as possible but with the proviso that if *I* consider any element of it to be unclear or ambiguous, then *I* shall ask supplementary questions myself, which you may answer publicly. Will that be acceptable?"

The foreman glanced at his fellow jurors who all appeared to nod. "Yes, your honour," he said.

"Then pray proceed."

The foreman drew himself up and took a deep breath: "We have concluded that, under the circumstances and in the light of all we have heard over the last few days, that an open verdict is the most appropriate in this case."

Lavenham-Burke raised an eyebrow: "Might this be because you entertain an inkling of sympathy for the notion that it may have been suicide?"

"No, your honour. We are entirely confident that the fatal blow was struck intentionally. But, whilst the fact that it was struck from behind might at first appear to rule out self-defence, there is always the possibility that the victim may have turned away at the last moment, thus receiving the blow from behind even though this may not have been the intention of the person who struck it. Nor does it rule out the possibility that the attacker was acting in defence of another, which – we believe – would be entirely consistent with evidence relayed to us by Mr Price."

"But would you go so far as to claim, thereby, that the victim was lawfully killed?" asked the Coroner.

"No your honour, we would not. Murder and manslaughter clearly remain possibilities, as do self defence and defence of another. For this reason we feel that an open verdict most reliably reflects the nature of the evidence we have seen and heard."

"Very well," said Mr Justice Lavenham-Burke. "That, then, is the verdict I shall record and endorse. It only remains for me to thank you all most sincerely – along with all witnesses of course - for your time and patience in this matter. I shall rise."

The court rose.

*

Early the following morning I drove over to Norwich to give Pete the news, though I suspected he had heard already via TV or radio. I found him sitting in the visitors' lounge with an attractive brunette I didn't immediately recognise.

"We have met," she said. "But I'm normally in uniform."

Of course. She was the nurse to whom I'd already suspected Peter had taken a shine. Looked like it was mutual.

"Evan," said Pete. "Meet Lizzy."

"It's my day off," she said. "We were thinking of going for a drive.

Want to come?"

I glanced at Peter: "You feel safe in a car after … well … you know … ?"

"Got to do it sooner or later," he shrugged.

It turned out Lizzy had access to one of the specially adapted vehicles belonging to the mobility unit, and Pete could easily slide into a mechanically lowered passenger seat. Rather to my surprise, he asked Lizzy if she thought we had enough time to get up to the coast and back.

"I need to see it all again. You know … where it … *happened*."

Lizzy glanced at her watch and pursed her lips.

"Yeah …" she said. "It's light till fourish and it's only ten thirty now. We can have lunch at that pub you told me about."

She caught my eye: "Oh … don't worry, I'll stick to lemonade!"

I still had O'Brien's cash in my rucksack as I didn't like to leave it lying around unattended and hadn't yet got round to banking it. (Perhaps I thought that to do something so conventional would look too much like I was keeping it for myself.) The truth was that I still had no idea *what* I was going to do with it. But as I climbed into a back seat and set it down beside me, I began to consider the question seriously for the first time since O'Brien had thrust it into my hands that wild and desperate night in *Samphire's* lamp-lit saloon.

As we pulled away from the suburbs of Norwich it struck me that – logically – I should be following in my own car, then I'd only have a short drive back to Hunswick at the end of the day. On the other hand, I'd just driven all the way *from* Hunswick and I deserved a break. So I sat back and enjoyed the view as we made our way cross country via little market towns such as Fakenham and Docking. Conversation – mostly between Lizzy and Pete - was sporadic, but I managed to deduce that her father was a chartered surveyor with a practise in Sherringham. I wondered if he was looking for a junior partner with recent experience of mapping a deceptive coastline, and a few minutes later it became apparent that he was.

We hit the coast at Chesterfleet and turned east along the A149. Eventually we slowed down through the bend where the crash had occurred.

"You okay, Pete?" asked Lizzy.

He nodded, but I could see in the rear-view mirror that he had closed his eyes. None of us spoke until we reached the *Aboukir Bay* some ten minutes later.

"Weird name," she remarked.

"Also known as the Battle of the Nile," I explained as we parked on the forecourt. I'd done my homework since August and it turned out my hunch about a Nelsonian victory had been correct.

"Of course!" she said. "Everyone reckons he learnt to sail around here, but I don't think there's any real evidence. Still, he *was* born just up the road so you never know."

Pete could just about manage with a pair of crutches now and we helped him up the steps into the bar, ordered drinks and asked for a menu. It was fairly quiet, which was perhaps unsurprising for a weekday in November, so we felt we could talk freely over our Stooky Blues and curried lobster. Even so I began to feel a little awkward. Neither Pete nor Lizzy had said or done anything to suggest it, but I knew I was gradually morphing into the proverbial gooseberry.

"Look ..." I said as the main courses were cleared away. "There's something I need to do. I'll meet you in front of the Chandlery in an hour or so. Or in the car if it's wet or too cold. Don't let me stop you having desert!"

Naturally they were a touch embarrassed and started to apologise profusely, but I think I managed to convince them I really needed to take a walk. At least I think I persuaded Pete, who knew me well enough to understand. Lizzy, poor girl, looked mortified. "I'm fine, honestly," I said, shrugging into the straps of my backpack, and flashing her what I hoped was a genuine smile. "See you later."

It was breezy out on the floodbank, with the occasional stinging shower of sleety rain. However, it was really quite mild in comparison with the conditions last time I'd walked this way. The saltmarsh was rust-coloured now, the sedge-tops rasping together in the wind. The few trees – mostly thorn – were stripped bare and clawed at the sky with arthritic fingers. An intricately convoluted network of puddles had appeared in the drained fields behind the banks, betraying the long lost channels which had once carried flood tides and even boats, perhaps, right up to the foot of the Downs. Geese grazed on the pale grass with the studious concentration of sheep or cattle. Others honked overhead in their long trembling skeins. The Kingdom of the East Angles, I thought, was looking its Spartan best.

I came to the point where the bank turned abruptly east, and paused. I turned and looked west, across Cockle Hole and up the length of the wide lagoon. A solitary yacht lay to her anchor exactly where we'd spent our first night at Boverey. Without binoculars I couldn't really determine her age or method of construction, but there was something homely and snug about the bright green tarp lashed, tent-like, over the boom. There was neither any light in the cabin nor any tender alongside.

Winter quarters, obviously.

A pit of longing opened in my abdomen. Never mind reacquainting myself with dinghies on reservoirs. Like *Samphire*, this was the real deal. Of course I may just have been channelling Mr Toad when he first set eyes on the yellow Gypsy caravan … or the shiny motor car that wrecked it!

Glancing beyond the boat I could see the weak winter sun illuminating the pale sand of the island beach, where I half expected to see a small red-headed Celt playing on the Saxon Shore. But of course the schools were back and the beaches were empty.

As before, I stepped off the floodbank and scrambled down into the hollow beneath the dunes. This time, though, I didn't struggle up to the summit of Battery Sand but climbed through a saddle of marram and seashells until I was on the vast north-facing beach. Here there was nothing to interrupt or divert the wind, which picked up long ropes of sand … plaiting and weaving them into granular, shape-shifting infinities barely distinguishable from the spindrift and the smoking waves.

I dumped my rucksack at my feet and stooped to open it. Gathering

Epilogue

a handful of pebbles from the foot of the dunes behind me, I unzipped the money bag and started to push the pebbles in amongst the notes. If I didn't want the money, he'd written, then I should throw it in the sea. To *want* the money seemed wrong … it simply wasn't mine. Though I could certainly use it: five grand would more than cover the deposit on the wreck of an old farmhouse I was interested in at the head of the Golden Valley back home … *and* go quite a way towards its restoration!

But no. It simply wasn't mine.

Striding towards the boiling surf, I hefted the package in my right hand, my arm swinging like a pendulum … higher and higher …

And then …

And then …

I froze … the bag hovering above my shoulder as if something or someone had grabbed my wrist. I had a sudden vision of myself as Abraham about to sacrifice his son … the angel staying his hand. Rembrandt's epic version flashed in front of me, and I remembered something Pete had said the night we'd sat up drinking Bushmills in the transit basin at Flitterby Sluice.

*

Peter and Lizzy were sitting on a bench in front of the Old Chandlery.

"You look like you've seen a ghost!" said Lizzy as I approached.

"No," I replied. "Only an angel."

She laughed somewhat coquettishly: "We get called that all the time in my job!"

"No! Sorry … I meant on the beach out there." I jerked my thumb back over my shoulder.

They glanced at each other, both frowning.

"You've done it, haven't you?" said Pete.

"Done what?"

"Thrown the money in the sea."

"What money?" Lizzy asked him, her face decidedly quizzical.

"Long story," I said. "But no. I haven't yet. But I *am* going to. At least I'm going to throw *half* of it into a hole in the water."

Lizzy's look of surprise ratcheted up into an expression of utter bewilderment. Pete, though, started to chuckle.

"As my uncle might have put it!" he laughed. "What about the other half?"

"An adoption charity, I think. As local to here as possible." I turned to Lizzy: "You wouldn't happen to know of such a thing, would you?"

"Not off hand," she said. "And I haven't the faintest idea what you're talking about, but I certainly know people who could help you out there. By the way, what was the angel actually *doing* on the beach?"

"Preventing Abraham from sacrificing Isaac."

"Well that brings back a few Sunday School memories!" she said. "Is that why you need an adoption charity?"

"In a funny sort of way," I said quietly. "*Indirectly* at least."

Peter glanced at his watch and up at the fading light: "Probably time we headed back."

"Just a moment," I said, noticing a glazed display board mounted on the Chandlery wall. Moving closer, I found it contained a number of curling, sun-bleached photographs of boats for sale.

"What is it?" asked Pete.

"Just looking for the right hole in the water," I said.

*

Retracing our route, we were soon passing through the empty, silent country between Docking and Fakenham. The fields were all ploughed now, and you could see patches of steely sky through the leafless woods where rooks' nests stood out like ink blots. We stopped at a T junction and a movement in the adjacent field caught my eye. About two hundred yards away a stooping figure was making its way along a thorn hedge. It paused and looked up: a bearded male wearing a dun-coloured coat with a cape of sacking draped over his shoulders. A black dog burst through a gap: big and shaggy. He bent down stroked it, then pulled something out of the hedge and rested it in the crook of his arm. A billhook.

We pulled away from the junction and a stack of hay bales shut off the view.

Lizzy must have caught my expression in the mirror.

"Seen another angel?" she asked.

"No," I replied. "Just a ghost this time."

A NOTICE TO MARINERS

(And Other Observations)

Anyone familiar with the Fenland rivers, the Wash, and the north Norfolk coast will have no difficulty identifying the principal locations of this story. The rivers and canals will not have changed very much since I wrote it (though I have taken some liberties around Flitterby Sluice) but the Wash and the North Sea are another matter entirely.

Please do *not* use this publication as a sailing guide! Sandbanks - even islands - come and go remarkably quickly here. Navigable channels can silt up almost overnight and new ones are blasted through the beaches and dunes with each storm-surge. (And the storm-surges do seem to be increasing in both frequency and ferocity.) The tidal range can be extreme: I once walked from Hunswick to Turnham using chart and compass, taking bearings on exposed seabed features, whilst the sea itself was invisible beyond the horizon!

If you do wish to explore this fascinating littoral by boat, and have access to a suitably robust, shoal-draughted vessel, I certainly wouldn't want to deter you. Just make sure you have bang-up-to-the-minute charts; brush up on your buoyage and lights and – above all – take advantage of local knowledge. Steve Holkham may be a fictional harbourmaster but he has his real equivalents all along this gloriously intricate coastline.

*

The law concerning Coroners' inquests is something which has certainly changed since I rolled page one into my typewriter.

Historically, an inquest jury could find that the deceased had been murdered by a named individual, which meant that the person concerned was effectively "tried" without having been either arrested or charged. A number of such cases between the wars engendered considerable public disquiet at this obviously dangerous custom. In 1929, for example, a touring American actor called Philip Yale Drew almost found himself on a British gallows when he was repeatedly named as the likely murderer of a Reading tobacconist. In the event, no actual charge was ever laid against Drew, but the experience had taken a terrible toll: his career never recovered and he died a broken man.

Various attempts were made to rectify this legal anomaly but – incredibly - there was nothing concrete until the Criminal Law Act of 1977. This was at least partially triggered by the recent inquest into the death of Sandra Rivett, nanny to the Lucan family. Here, the Coroner's jury had declared openly that the victim had been murdered by the vanished Lord Lucan himself. In point of fact, the empanelling of Coroners' juries was actually quite rare by the 1970s. Now it is almost unheard of.

The *three mile limit*, referred to in the discussion concerning the circumstances in which an inquest into a death at sea may be held, was extended to twelve miles in 1987. I am not yet clear whether Brexit will affect this either way.

Watkyn de Snettisham is purely a figment of my imagination, though the battling bishop was real enough. As for Black Shuck, I believe I *may* once have seen him prowling a quiet lane near Walsingham …